QUEEN OF THE FAE

DRAGON'S GIFT: THE DARK FAE BOOK 3

LINSEY HALL

For Amanda.

1

The Thorn Wolf stared at me from his place in front of the fireplace, yellow eyes glowing.

"You doing all right, pal?" I stirred a droplet of blood into a potion that simmered in a small onyx bowl.

Bacon.

"Hmmmm. I can tell by your tone that you're peeved."

He harrumphed.

"I don't think he's all that keen on Wally," Aeri said from her position on the other side of the table.

I eyed the little hellcat who had curled up on top of Burn's thorny back. Wally was a creature of the underworld, a little black cat with smoking fur and fire for eyes. He was Aeri's sidekick, and he was just as murderous as Burn when he felt like it.

But apparently, what he felt like *now* was using my wolf as a mattress.

And the wolf was not pleased.

Or at least, he was pretending to not be pleased. I thought he secretly liked Wally.

"Maybe you can bond by murdering demons together," I said to him. "It works for me and Aeri."

"And if all else fails, have a cocktail." Aeri grinned at the two creatures, never letting up on the perfect rhythm with which she stirred the potion in front of her.

It'd been only a day since we'd fixed the massive crevasse that I'd blown into the earth in Magic's Bend, and we were back at it in our workshop, brewing some potion bombs for the fight to come. My mother was after me, and she wasn't going to be nice about it. I'd tried to use my new Unseelie power of premonition to see exactly what she was planning, but it wasn't that easy to control.

Basically, I was still in the dark. And it was frustrating as hell.

"How are you coming?" I asked her.

"Almost done. We'll be up to twenty acid bombs in no time."

"Excellent." It was nice to have a short break from the fighting. A very short break, given that I only had today. For our little potion-making party, I'd worn one of my usual black plunging gowns, and it felt good to be dressed like myself again. Not that my fight wear wasn't me—it could be argued that it was even more my style—but I liked the break.

I eyed the clock. Just two hours to go.

"You've looked at that clock five times in the last ten minutes," Aeri said. "That excited?"

"I'm not sure that excited is the word for it." My heart fluttered, betraying my lie.

"Sure, sure. The hot Fae king is coming over, and you're not even a *little* excited."

"He's coming over to help me hunt down my murderous mother because he is bent on getting vengeance for his dead brother." I grimaced, fairly convinced that his quest for vengeance was the main reason he spent any time around me. Especially since I'd spent basically all my time lying to him about something or other. Usually something giant. "So yeah, not exactly a great start to a relationship."

"No one said being fated mates is easy."

"Truer words," I muttered, setting down the obsidian blade with which I stirred my potion.

Despite our issues, the fated mate bond was hard to resist. We were like two trains hurtling toward each other. No brakes. The path was getting bumpy, but we weren't slowing down.

At the hearth, Burn started to growl. The low rumble was a sound I only heard in battle. Wally lifted his head, too, flame eyes blinking. He hissed, back arching.

"What's wrong, guys? Do you—"

A massive explosion from behind threw me forward, cutting off my words. I slammed into the table, the hard wooden edge gouging my stomach. The potion in the stone bowl soaked the front of my dress, burning slightly. Aeri was thrown back against the wall.

My heart thundered and pain flared in my stomach as I

shoved myself upright, whirling around.

The entire side wall of our workshop had been blown away, revealing the back garden through a haze of rubble and smoke. A slender, unfamiliar figure approached through the mist. I darted right to get some cover, drawing my bow and arrow from the ether.

"Who the hell are you?" I raised my bow and fired, but the figure darted to the right, easily avoiding my shot.

Shit.

From the corner of my eye, I caught sight of Aeri, groaning as she dragged herself to her feet.

Burn and Wally lunged forward, snarls erupting from their throats and fangs bared.

The figure threw out his hand, and a blast of wind slammed the two animals back into the wall.

Rage lit in my chest.

"You bastard." I raised my bow to fire again, but the stranger was fast. He hurled something at me. It glinted red in the firelight as it flew, and I lunged left, narrowly avoiding the potion bomb. It smashed into the wall behind me, leaving a smoking red solution dripping down the paint.

I fired again, and he darted left so fast he avoided my arrow.

Shit.

Finally, he stepped through the smoke, his features becoming apparent.

Pale skin, sharp cheekbones, black eyes.

And wings.

Fae wings.

"Unseelie," I hissed.

"So are you." The grin he gave me bordered on evil. His magic reeked of sulfur and rot.

Aeri charged, swinging her mace in an arc overhead to get up the speed required for a kill. She loosened the chain to hit him from afar, but he ducked at the last minute, insanely fast.

Even faster than Aeri and me. We had enhanced speed, thanks to our Dragon Blood, and it was rare we met someone quicker.

My mother had sent someone equipped to take us out.

No way in hell I'd let that happen.

Aeri swung her mace right for his head. The spikes of the metal ball scraped through his hair, and he hissed, black eyes flashing. He threw out his hand again and sent another blast of wind at her. It picked her up and threw her back against the wall. She hit hard, thudding, then slid to the ground.

I fired another arrow, adjusting my attack to assume he would dodge right. He did, and my flying arrow hit him in the shoulder so his arm hung limp. He howled and raised a potion bomb in his good hand, hurling it at me.

I dived right, narrowly avoiding the strike.

To my left, Aeri leapt up and threw a dagger at the Unseelie. He darted left, but it hit him in the side. He hissed, yanking out the steel blade as fast as he could and throwing another strong blast of wind at Aeri, who slammed back into the wall again, cracking the plaster.

Burn and Wally growled and lunged forward.

I threw out a hand. "Back, guys!"

Their fangs wouldn't do enough damage to this guy. Not unless they could coat them with steel.

Hey, that's a good idea.

"More steel," I said to Aeri. The Fae were extra sensitive to it. Being half Fae protected me from the worst of the iron burn, but I still didn't love it.

I raised my bow once more, calling on an arrow with a steel tip. As I fired, he threw a third potion bomb at me.

Instinct made me abandon my shot and dive out of the way of the potion bomb. He was so accurate this time that I heard it whiz by my head.

All potion bombs were bad, but there was something about these that made me extra wary.

For one, he was only sending potions at me.

Did he know that I had a new Unseelie magic? I could absorb and return magical assaults. And though I hadn't tested it, I sincerely doubted my skills worked with potions.

"You're going to run out of those." I shot upright and fired, my arrow nearly hitting his shoulder. He darted, and I fired again, using my Dragon Blood speed to my advantage.

Nailed it.

The arrow hit him in the other shoulder, and he howled.

I fired again, aiming for the bag hanging at his side. My arrow slammed into it, shattering the contents.

He growled, reaching for it.

"No more left, huh?"

Hatred flashed on his face, and he turned and ran.

Burn sprinted after him, unable to resist the chase. Quickly, I looked toward Aeri, who was dragging herself upright.

"Go." Her eyes flashed.

I raced after the Unseelie. He was my only connection to my mother. Tarron and I planned to try to access the Unseelie Court through the Circle of Night again, but we sincerely doubted it was still open.

This could be my only lead.

I leapt over the rubble of the destroyed wall, sprinting past hundreds of broken bottles of ingredients. The loss made my stomach turn. Not only was this stuff expensive, some of it was incredibly hard to come by. This bastard had set us *way* back in our Blood Sorcery business. As I ran outside, I called upon my new Unseelie wings.

Burn stood in the yard, growling at the sky. I looked up, spotting the Unseelie overhead. His black wings looked ragged and worn, but they carried him swiftly away from my house.

I launched myself into the air, grateful for how much easier flying had become ever since I'd visited the Unseelie Court to complete the ritual that all Unseelie went through to unite the magic within them.

Wind tore at my dress and hair as I flew after the Unseelie. I chased him over the rooftops, the setting sun watching our progress. The view was totally different from up here, and I thanked fates that Magic's Bend was an all supernatural city.

The damned Unseelie was fast, and far more practiced with his wings than I. He flew down into narrow alleys, cutting around corners and trying to elude me.

I pushed myself, wings aching and lungs burning. No way I'd lose this bastard now. It was early evening, right after work got out for most, and some of the streets were packed with people. The Unseelie cut close to their heads, flying low. Shouts and curses followed him.

Near Factory Row, he reached a park. There were no people I could spot, so I drew a dagger from the ether and hurled it at him. The blade sank into the corner of his wing, and he faltered, shrieking.

I put on a burst of speed and collided with him, taking him down through the trees. Branches dragged at my hair and dress as we fell, and I barely managed to force us to rotate so he hit the ground first.

He slammed into the grass with a grunt, and his elbow went into my stomach. The air whooshed out of me, and I temporarily lost my grip. He tried to scramble upward, but I lunged for him, pinning him down.

I called on a steel dagger from the ether. Ruthlessly, I pressed the dagger against his ribs, making sure that the point broke the skin.

He flinched and turned white. "She wants you," he hissed. "She'll stop at nothing."

"Tell me where she is."

He spat at me.

I ducked left, barely dodging. I dug the dagger deeper into his skin. "Tell me, or I'll gut you."

"You'll do that anyway."

I grinned viciously. "Normally, yes. But I quite like the idea of sending you back to my mother with a message. *If you tell me where I can find her.*"

"Never."

"Fine, then." I sliced my fingertip with my thumbnail, enjoying the slight bite of pain. "I'll make you."

I raised my bloody fingertip to his forehead, ready to swipe it against his skin and use my Dragon Blood magic to force him to tell me.

"Just go to her," he said. "Or we'll keep coming for you."

"I'll go to her on my terms." Until I knew I could resist her mind control magic, I couldn't go to her. With my power, it'd be like putting a nuclear bomb in her hands.

I raised my hand to swipe my fingertip across his forehead.

Before I could reach him, his hand shot up, and he smashed something against my arm. Glass shattered.

Potion bomb.

The thought registered in my mind in a flash. I reached up and tore the sleeve off my dress, yanking it down my arm before the potion could soak through to my skin.

Cool air drifted over a small patch on my arm.

Dread uncoiled within me as I looked down. A bit of red liquid stained my arm.

The Unseelie laughed, an unsettling sound.

Apparently, I hadn't destroyed all of his bombs.

His hand swiped up, and he touched my arm, sending a bolt of energy into my mind. My magic twined with his as my vision began to go white. A buzzing started in my head, louder and louder.

I stiffened, losing my grip on the blade. Through the last of my clear vision, I spotted Aeri racing up to me. Cass, as well, coming from across the street where her shop was located.

"Go to her, or the flames will burn." His words were the last thing I heard before the premonition sucked me in.

I collapsed to the ground beside the Unseelie. Panic flared in my chest as everything went white inside my mind, fluffy clouds surrounding me. Just like in my trials.

Except this had something to do with my mother and her minions. I could feel it.

Gasping, I spun in a circle, alive inside my mind.

I knew what to do.

I'd been practicing.

I drew in a deep breath to force away the panic and focused on the concept of *truth*.

She was sending me a message, and I needed to see it. Something tugged at me from the left, and I knew it was my mother.

This was a vision she was sending me. It had to be.

I ran toward her signature, my heart pounding.

As the mist cleared, flame took its place.

Horror threatened to swallow me whole.

I was gazing upon the Seelie Court and kingdom—

there was no mistaking the ornate architecture and beautiful inhabitants.

Terrible flames raced down the street, chasing people from their homes as they devoured the buildings. The fire flickered orange, blue, and green. Magic sparkled at the tips of the flame.

It would destroy the entire kingdom and everyone in it.

Come to me. Somehow, her voice echoed in my mind. *Come to me, and all of this can be stopped.*

There was no way. I was a Dragon Blood—capable of making any magic in the world. The equivalence of a nuclear bomb. If my mother got ahold of my mind like she had the last time, she could do far worse than destroy the Seelie kingdom.

She could destroy the whole world.

At the edges of the blaze, my mother's dark smoke crept along the ground. It was the same magic that had possessed my mind and body when I'd seen her last. It was the magic that kept her in control in the Unseelie realm. It had to be. She could possess anyone she got close enough to.

And she was doing it to the Seelie.

The ones who weren't burning were turning toward her side.

She was a madwoman.

I could feel it in the air—her desire to destroy and possess. It was like we had some kind of horrible connection. She had failed to turn the Seelie to her side with the crystal obelisk, so she was going to burn the place to the ground and capture the minds of anyone lucky enough to survive.

Though lucky wasn't necessarily the word I'd use if they ended up under her spell.

I had to stop her.

But how?

My head ached as I called upon a vision of a future where I could stop her. A future where I could change all this.

Was it even possible?

The vision came easily—more easily than any vision I'd ever had.

And it sent me to my knees.

Again, I saw myself plunging a blade into Tarron's chest.

I'd had this vision once before, so recently that it was still fresh in my mind. Me, weeping, while I killed Tarron.

I hadn't told him.

I hadn't wanted it to be true.

Yet here I was, seeing it again.

And this time, it was the solution to the horror that my mother planned for the entire Seelie kingdom. It was difficult to see the details, but there was no mistaking the blade that plunged into his flesh or the tears on my face. This was no trick of the light.

If I wanted to save the thousands of Seelie who were burning in front of my eyes, I would have to kill Tarron.

Their king. My fated mate.

2

"Mari! Wake up!" Aeri's voice cut through the fog in my mind.

She shook me hard, rattling my brain as I sat up, blinking. My gaze moved to the dead Fae next to me. Someone had plunged a steel blade through the Unseelie's chest. Black smoke curled up from the seeping wound.

Burn stood over the Fae, eying the bloody neck that he'd clearly just torn apart. Black blood dripped from his fangs, and his muzzle was pulled back in a growl.

The Fae's hair smoked, charred to the skull. Wally, the fire-breathing hellcat who followed my sister around, had clearly done his own bit of damage. The little beast sat nearby, cleaning his inky black paws.

It was still dark out, and the cool night air blew my sweaty hair back from my forehead. Aeri sat over me, gripping my arms tight. Cass stood behind her, concern in her green eyes.

My gaze flashed up to Aeri. "Did you kill him?"

"No. He did it to himself when he saw us coming." She gestured back to Cass. "Twisted the blade right in his own heart. Then Burn got excited and lunged. Wally followed."

"Damn." I'd wanted to keep interrogating him.

"Are you all right?" Cass asked. "I saw you fall from the sky while I was closing up my shop."

"It was more of a dive, but yeah, I'm fine." I drew a shaky hand across my forehead, unable to stop the trembling.

This wasn't like me.

My arm.

The memory flashed in my mind. I looked down at the smear of red potion that stained my pale skin. Thin veins of black ran through the liquid.

"You saw a vision, didn't you?" Aeri asked.

Shakily, I nodded. "How could you tell?"

"You kept muttering stuff like 'no' and 'not true.'"

The horrible image flashed in front of my mind again, and I closed my eyes. "He hit me with one of the potion bombs. Just a little bit got on me, but it was enough to help direct my premonition sense."

"What do you mean?" Aeri asked.

"I think my mother sent me a vision."

Aeri's gaze was riveted to my arm, then to the torn sleeve that I'd flung away. It lay on the grass.

"Let's go to P & P," Cass said. "You can get some water, and Connor can figure out whatever was in that potion that the Fae hit you with."

Connor was a potions master as well as the owner of our favorite bar, Potions & Pastilles.

"And you look like you need something stronger than water," Aeri said.

"That's the truth," Cass said.

I grinned wearily, then looked at the Thorn Wolf. "Burn, go guard the house, would you?"

He woofed low in his throat, then disappeared. Wally followed.

Our house might have a hole blown in the back wall, but if Burn and Wally were guarding it, no one would get in.

"I'm going to head back to my place to get something to take care of this bastard." Cass nudged the Fae's still foot.

"You're the best." I smiled at her. Unlike the demons we normally killed in our day jobs, Unseelie Fae bodies didn't just disappear. Having a friend to do the dirty cleanup work—before any cops showed up—was worth a million bucks.

Cass saluted. "Any time, pal."

She loped off toward the warm golden lights of P & P and her shop. Both were located right across from the park and a few doors down from each other.

"Come on." Aeri helped me stand. "Let's get you to P & P."

We could possibly do it at home as well—neither of us was a slouch with potions—but Connor was particularly good at this sort of thing. He'd probably be faster, too, especially since most of our ingredients were smashed beneath the broken wall.

"The vision was bad, Aeri." I couldn't help but play it over in my mind.

"Tell me all about it over some coffee and a pasty."

My stomach growled, and I grimaced, my gaze going to the body next to me. Connor's famous Cornish pasties were a rare treat, and apparently I hadn't eaten in a while. "Yeah. Let's go."

I found my stilettos, which had fallen off in the fight. One had a broken heel. "Damn it. I liked that pair."

I picked up the stilettos, which were midnight black with silver spikes all over them. I used the heel of the unbroken one to scoop up the torn sleeve, not wanting to touch it with my bare skin.

Aeri helped me across the grass. I spotted Cass locking up her shop, and she passed us on her way back to the body, a big bag slung over her shoulder.

She stopped briefly. "I don't know what to do with this guy, so just send me a message if you want him for any reason."

"Check if he's got something that will help locate the queen of the Unseelie," I said. "Otherwise, just get rid of him."

"On it."

"You're the best. I owe you one."

"You've had my back plenty. Payback time." She raced off, and Aeri and I continued on.

We crossed the street and entered P & P, which was

nearly empty save for a few old men huddled around a table drinking golden whiskey. The rush would come soon, once people made it from the Business District to this side of town for a night out.

The warm interior smelled of pastries and whiskey, an excellent evening combination. Golden light shined from mason jar lamps that hung on wires from the ceiling. Warm wood glowed under their light, and local art decorated the walls. It was a trendy, hipster place, with unrecognizable but pleasant music playing on the speakers.

Connor looked up from behind the counter, his floppy dark hair swept over his forehead. He grinned and waved. Today, his band T-shirt proclaimed him a fan of Worakles, which I'd never heard of. But then, Connor had broad taste in music.

His sister, Claire, pushed through the door behind the counter, coming from the kitchen in the back. She wore her black fighting leathers and had a streak of blood across her face.

"You're going to have to clean up if you're working tonight," Connor said.

Claire grinned at him. "Consider it my night off."

"Ha-ha. As if." Connor flicked some water at his sister.

Claire was a mercenary for the Order of the Magica, one of the supernatural governments. She helped out at P & P occasionally, but it was primarily Connor's baby. He was a hearth witch and potions master, which made him perfect for the gig.

He sighed and turned to us. "She'll be the death of me."

"Whatever, bro." Claire grinned at us, then frowned. "You okay? Looking paler than normal, Mordaca."

"Yeah. I'm good. Fantastic, really."

"Liar. Let me know if you need anything." She disappeared through the door, back into the kitchen.

I thanked fates for my amazing friends. We weren't very close—not all mushy or anything; that wasn't my style—but we did understand each other. All of us had secrets so none of us pried. But when we needed help—body cleanup, demon disposal—we could count on each other.

Aeri and I approached the counter, and Connor's gaze went from my bare feet to the shoes and torn sleeve in my hand. "Busy night?"

"You could say that." I held up the shoes so the material dangled higher in the air. "I was hit by a potion bomb that soaked into my sleeve. Could you identify it?"

He nodded. "Sure."

I raised my arm, indicating the red stain of potion. "And mind if I use your bathroom?"

He gestured to the corner where the door was located. "Help yourself. I'll tell Claire to get you something to eat."

"Thanks." I handed over the sleeve, and he disappeared into the back. His potions workshop was located past the kitchen.

I straightened, pulling away from Aeri and walking under my own steam to the bathroom. I might have been shell-shocked by the vision, but weakness wasn't my style. And if there was one thing I had, it was style.

I stepped into the tiny bathroom, grimacing at the feel of the cold tile on my bare feet. Though I dealt with gross things like demon blood on a daily basis, walking into a public restroom without shoes was *so* not my idea of a good time.

"Just add it to the list of shitty things in a shitty day," I muttered.

At least Connor kept the place clean.

Quickly, I scrubbed off the red potion that stained my arm. Besides the weird vision, I felt mostly normal. Unfortunately, that didn't mean anything as far as potions were concerned. They could be slow-acting. Or subtle.

One minute you'd be walking around; the next, you could be dead.

Also not my idea of a good time.

Cleaned up, I consulted my reflection.

Ragged.

Ew.

This would *not* do.

I waved a hand in front of my face, using a glamour to fix the appearance of my hair and dress. I was still technically a mess, but no one could tell. I couldn't do anything about my broken shoes, but I made sure that the illusion of my black dress went all the way to the floor. Finally looking like myself again, I returned to the coffee shop and joined Aeri in the comfy chairs in the corner.

We sat, and Aeri leaned close. "What did you see in the vision?"

I drew in a deep breath and described the burning town, along with my mother's black magic infecting the minds of the Seelie. And finally, the image of me killing Tarron.

"What?" Shock dropped Aeri's jaw.

"Exactly. She's enraged—she failed to capture the Seelie kingdom before, so now she wants to destroy it."

"You're sure it's true?"

"Definitely. The only question is, can I change it?"

"You've got to ask Aethelred."

"That's what I was thinking." The old seer was one of my few close friends.

Except, that wasn't quite true, was it? I seemed to have a lot of friends these days. But Aethelred was one of the oldest. When things weren't completely crazy, we met every Friday for a morning walk along the beach so we could gossip. He had to bribe me with bacon sandwiches to get up that early, but for him, I did it. Though we made a weird pair, I loved him.

"Why did your mother send you the vision? Couldn't it give you enough time to stop her?"

"It could. I don't think she realized that I could read her intentions in the premonition. It was like we were connected. Nothing will stop her, not even if I go to her. But she showed me the vision to threaten me into coming to her, promising to stop it if I did."

"Ha." Aeri gave a bitter laugh. "She can dream right on with that."

"Right?" Many supernaturals would think it was great to be able to create any magic with a few drops of blood—or more blood, if you wanted the power to be permanent. But the truth was, I lived my life in fear of being used as a weapon.

It had happened before, to both me and Aeri. Not only had Aunt tried to use us as weapons, but after we'd escaped her clutches, our first friend in the real world had turned us over to the Order of the Magica. We'd barely escaped, but the experience had been formative, to say the least.

"I have to stop my mother to save Tarron. It's the only way. Because whatever she's going to do can only be fixed with his death. The vision was clear on that."

"How is that possible?"

"I have no idea. I couldn't see details, but that bit was clear."

Claire appeared at our table, her face scrubbed clean and her dark hair wet from a quick shower. She was now dressed in jeans and a T-shirt, with a little black apron slung around her waist. She set a tray on the table. "Compliments of the house. Connor's working on your potion."

"Thanks."

She smiled, but there were shadows in her eyes.

"Bad day?" I asked.

"Not a fun job." She shivered. "Sometimes being a mercenary sucks."

I didn't tell her to get a new job. Claire knew what she was about, even if it left scars.

I squeezed her hand, a rare show of affection. I wasn't much of a toucher, and she knew it.

"Thanks." She smiled, then disappeared.

I ignored the steaming espresso and savory pastry that sat on the tray. "Give me a moment."

I closed my eyes, calling upon my gift. I'd done this two dozen times before, trying to see my mother. To figure out what she was up to and how I could stop her. Maybe I could see something else based on the vision she'd sent me.

Nothing came to me.

"Shit." I opened my eyes. "When I try, I can't see anything."

"She's a powerful Fae. She may be blocked from you."

"Hopefully Aethelred can see something that I can't." The seer was massively powerful, and though he didn't see all, what he did see was true. I prayed that my power worked differently—that I saw potential futures. Not the one true future.

"Eat," Aeri commanded. "Once Connor tells us what was in that potion bomb, we need to go fix our house."

I swigged back the espresso and picked up the pasty. The half-moon shaped pastry was full of savory filling—beef and potatoes in this case. The traditional version. It was a classic back in Cornwall, where Claire and Connor had come from. They'd made it a specialty at P & P, and pretty much everyone in town was a fan.

I was just finishing the pastry when Connor came out of the back, his face set in concerned lines.

"Shit," I muttered. Quickly, I unwrapped a butterscotch and shoved it in my mouth.

Aeri turned and frowned. "Double shit. Connor doesn't usually look so dire."

From the expression on his face, this was going to be bigger than butterscotch. Stress tugged at me, tightening my muscles.

He joined us and sat in one of the cushy chairs, leaning forward and propping his hands on his knees. "It's a mind control potion."

I'd feared as much when I'd seen the black stripes running through the red. My mother's mind control magic worked like a black smoke that filled your lungs and polluted your mind.

"How bad?" I asked.

"Strong. Very. But I think its efficacy depends on quantity. You got that sleeve off quickly, so it shouldn't be too strong. For now."

"So the influence could grow? It could get worse?"

"Could. Definitely don't get hit with another dose. One more and whoever made this potion bomb will be your master."

I grimaced. "I'll try not to."

I leaned back in the chair. Shit. My mother was trying to work her mind control even from a distance. It had probably allowed the Unseelie to send me the vision.

I rubbed my arms, feeling weird. Like there were

spiders in my head, or something. Some kind of horrible, unfamiliar force that could strike at any time.

"Is there an antidote?" Aeri asked.

"Not one that I'm familiar with."

"The antidote will be killing my mother," I muttered.

Connor grimaced. "Family drama?"

"You could put it that way."

"Well, I'll see if I can come up with another antidote. Just in case you need it."

"Thanks, you're the best."

He nodded, then stood. "Good luck."

As he walked back to the counter, Aeri left a wad of cash on the table. It was far more than our food would have cost.

"A thank you," she said.

Connor had helped us because he liked us, but we liked to make things even. In this case, since we were busy, it would have to be with cash.

"Let's get out of here," I said. "I'm running out of time."

I was supposed to meet Tarron that evening so we could get started hunting for my mother again, and there were things I wanted to do beforehand.

I walked out onto the street. Aeri followed, and we headed toward Ancient Magic. On a normal night, it would be closed by now. But Cass was kindly dealing with the body of the Unseelie.

I pulled open the glass door of the shop and stepped inside. The cluttered little space was full of magic, as usual, and Cass sat behind the counter, clutching an obsidian dagger in her hand. She'd slung her brown leather jacket over the counter and was dressed in a white T-shirt that looked like it had seen better days.

"That came from the Unseelie, huh?" I asked, eying the dagger she held. They'd all carried the black volcanic glass daggers when I'd visited their realm.

"Yep." She frowned down at the thing. "But it's not giving me any insight to jump-start my ability. It was the only thing he carried that might do it, too."

Damn it. Cass's ability to find things far outstripped my Seeker ability. "We'll just have to hope the Circle of Night isn't closed."

She raised a brow. "You're going to try it?"

I shrugged. "I was hoping I'd be able to use my new gift of premonition to find my mother, but it hasn't worked. So the circle is our only clue right now."

"There could be an ambush."

"Probably will be."

"Want backup?"

I smiled. "Wouldn't hate it."

She nodded. "I'll get Nix and Del, so we'll have plenty."

"Thanks. I think we'll go at dawn. It's when it's most likely to be open."

We arranged a meeting point, then parted ways. This would work well with Tarron arriving soon. I used my transport magic, taking Aeri back to our place. We arrived on the sidewalk right in front of our main door.

"You'd never know the wall was blown in," I said.

"Seriously."

We hurried into the house and went straight back to the workshop. It still looked like hell, but there appeared to be a new wall where none had been prior. I walked up to it, careful to avoid any sparkling glass that shined on the floor, and stuck my hand right through.

"Nice work," I said.

"Thanks."

Burn stuck his thorny head through the illusion of the wall and woofed.

"Anyone give you trouble while we were gone?" I asked.

Bacon.

"That means no," I translated for Aeri.

"I'll deal with this mess while you talk to Aethelred," Aeri said.

"Thanks." I squeezed her shoulder as I passed her and strode to my apartment. Quickly, I changed into my fight wear. There was no more time for dresses and heels. The reprieve had been nice, though it had only lasted a few minutes before the damned Unseelie had shown up and I was shoved back into the fight.

Dressed, I looked into the mirror. My makeup was still impeccable—a handy talent of mine—and the black mask of paint obscured much of the area around my eyes. I patted the small bouffant on top, then pulled the rest into a ponytail.

Ready—and most importantly, now wearing shoes—I headed out to the foyer.

The knock on the door made the hair at my neck stand on end. Awareness prickled along my spine.

I'd heard that knock before.

Tarron.

He was early. I drew in a shuddery breath.

I was definitely not ready.

3

I strode to the door and swung it open, revealing the devastatingly handsome Fae king on the other side. He towered over me, even more so than usual because I wasn't wearing my stilettos. His broad shoulders blocked my view of the street beyond, and he was dressed for battle in sturdy black clothes that would conceal blood and allow for flexibility.

I appreciated a good fighter, and damned if he wasn't one.

Dark hair framed his face, and his green eyes were keen on me. He had that otherworldly beauty of the Fae, but with a distinctly masculine edge. A dangerous edge, one that made it clear he was capable of terrible things when necessary. It made him just a little bit scary.

I happened to like scary.

Tension tightened the air between us, that kind of intense awareness that came when you were near a person you wanted to jump on. In a tear-their-clothes-off kind of way.

Except that our chemistry was tainted with lies.

My lies, mostly.

We'd seen each other less than twenty-four hours ago.

Together, we'd closed the huge chasm that I'd blown into the earth at the edge of Magic's Bend. He'd figured out that I'd been hiding the fact that my mother was the Unseelie queen.

So yeah, we were fated mates, but things weren't exactly going smoothly.

It didn't keep me from wanting him, even though I knew he was only here to hunt my mother. He wanted vengeance for his brother's death, and he'd stop at nothing to get it.

His gaze swept over me, and from the heat that entered his eyes, he seemed to like what he saw. "You look like you're ready to fight."

I gestured down to my tight black pants. "Not my preferred attire, but it will do for what's ahead." I gave him a searching look. "I wasn't expecting you quite yet."

Concern flashed in his gaze as it traveled over me. "I could feel that something was wrong."

Yeah, that was putting it mildly.

The fated mate bond must have alerted him.

My instinct was to brush it all off and say everything was fine. Superficial relationships were my speed. Even my close friendships with Cass, Connor, and Claire were based more on common life experience than me baring my soul to them.

"It's nothing," I said.

Suspicion flickered in his eyes.

Shit, that had been stupid. I was keeping enough things from him. I didn't need to add something stupid to it. Old habits died hard, and all that.

"I was hit by a potion bomb sent by my mother." I relayed what Connor had said about it. "And I had a vision about her plans for the future."

His dark brows rose. "Really?"

"Flames. Lots and lots of flames." I described what I'd seen, leaving out the part about killing him to stop her. My stomach rolled as I thought of it.

That bit barely made any sense, and I was going to stop it from happening, so it didn't matter.

Baby steps, right?

Still, guilt tugged at me.

"Give me a moment," he said. "I need to inform the Court Guard of this risk. I want them to begin preparations to protect the realm."

I wasn't sure what they could do about fire, but I waited while he stepped back into the street and made a quick call on a discrete comms charm strapped to his wrist.

He returned to the doorway a few moments later. "Where are you headed now?"

"I need to find out how to stop my mother. I've been trying my premonition power, but it doesn't always come when I call. So I'm headed to Aethelred's. He's a local seer I hope can help."

"I'll come with you."

Great. Not what I'd been hoping for. "Sure."

Together, we left the house, and I took a right. "He's just a few doors down."

The sun had set, and the street was bustling with the denizens of Darklane. They were creatures of the night, these people. Like me.

"It smells of dark magic here," Tarron said.

I shrugged. "Not too much."

In truth, I'd grown used to it. After all, Darklane wasn't totally evil. Just a little bit. A very little bit. And not because of me.

We approached Aethelred's building and climbed the steps. I knocked, using the signature beat three fast and two slow.

"Mordaca?" His voice filtered through the door, and I could imagine him hurrying through the cluttered hall.

"It's me!"

The door swung open to reveal an ancient man with a long white beard and piercing blue eyes. He wore a matching blue velour tracksuit and looked like Gandalf on his way to aerobics. It was his usual uniform.

"Hey, Aethelred." I smiled. "We need some help."

He sized up Tarron. "Who's the big fellow?"

Tarron held out his hand. "Alexander. Elemental mage."

Liar. It was the same alias he'd used with me when I'd

first met him, and I'd let him keep it. I needed to stay on his good side, after all.

Aethelred shook and frowned. "You're not called Alexander."

"You're a good seer."

He shrugged. "What I see is true, Tarron, King of the Seelie Fae."

Tarron inclined his head.

"Can we come in?" I asked. "We're in a hurry."

"What's the rush?"

"We're trying to stop the destruction of the entire Seelie kingdom," I said.

Aethelred harrumphed. "At least it's not Magic's Bend. This town has seen too many emergencies, lately. I'm too old for it."

I grimaced. The last one had been my fault.

He shook his head, then gestured for us to follow him. "Come in, come in. We'll make this quick."

I followed him through the narrow hall, into his darkened living room. The blinds were partially drawn so light filtered through, and the space was cluttered with all sorts of random stuff, from books to trinkets and even a crystal that glowed as bright as the moon. The furniture was ancient and dusty, and when we sat on the couch, little dust motes floated up and glittered in the light of the lamps.

Aethelred took a chair and leaned toward me. "Now tell me what you want to know."

I smiled gratefully at him. Normally, he'd demand

payment, just like I would. He'd even be a stickler about whether or not he was willing to help.

But not with me.

"Thanks, Aethelred." I needed to get him alone to ask about Tarron, but I had to be subtle. I started by describing my new gift of premonition, and finished with my vision of flames and my mother's dark smoke. "Could you confirm that it is true? Did I really see the future, or is it just a threatening vision that she sent me?"

He nodded, then held out his hands. I reached for them and gripped them gently.

"Clear your mind so that you see what you saw before." His voice droned low.

I sucked in a slow breath and did as he asked. The image flared to mind.

Aethelred's power flowed into me, and a few moments later, he released my hand and opened his eyes. Tension tugged at me. His gaze flicked between me and Tarron, concern in their blue depths. Was it truly the future? Or had he seen that I could kill Tarron to stop this terrible fate?

The old seer drew in a deep breath. "I can see the past here, and a bit of motivation. She seeks to destroy the Seelie, and it has something to do with you, my dear. She tried to sway them to her side before. With a failed plan of some sort."

"The obelisk," I clarified, leaving out any mention of Tarron's brother.

"Ah, yes. That must have been it." Aethelred nodded. "It failed, and now she seeks to destroy them."

"So it could happen?" Tarron said.

"Yes. It could."

"*Could*?" Tarron asked. "It's not definite? It could be stopped, then?"

"Perhaps." Aethelred shrugged, looking uncertain. "This was a vision of Mordaca's. I don't know how her magic works. She may see the one true future like I do, or she may see potential futures that can be changed."

I swallowed hard, not wanting to contemplate how the tragedy would be stopped. I didn't even understand *how* killing Tarron would stop it. What was the connection there?

"Can you see how to stop it?" Tarron asked.

I gave Aethelred the tiniest shake of my head.

His blue eyes flashed, but the tone of his voice didn't change. "I cannot."

"I've tried to see more," I said. "Like when it will happen or how exactly she'll do it, but I've had no luck."

"You're new at it." He shook his head, blue eyes alight. "Marvelous that you have a new power."

"Several. Except they aren't cooperating."

"Practice, child. That's what you need. And when the visions don't come, it can help to find something to give them a little push."

Just like how Cass's FireSoul ability to find things was stronger if she had an object related to what she was seeking. "Give it a little push how, exactly?"

"If you want to see more about the Unseelie queen or what she will do, then find something of hers. Or go to a place that is important to her. It could give your magic a bit of gasoline. Send it in the right direction."

I had nothing of hers except myself—and I hated the idea that I was in any way hers.

"The Circle of Night," Tarron said. "It's as close as we can get to their realm."

"And we were planning to go anyway, since it's our only link to her," I said.

"That's the ticket," Aethelred said. "You're closest to this, so you're most likely to be the one to see how to fix it."

"I hope you're right."

He harrumphed. "I'm always right." He stood. "Now come with me. I have something I must ask you about."

I stood, and Tarron shifted as if to join me.

"Not you, young man." Aethelred waved him down. "This is for Mordaca alone."

Tarron sat back down, seeming curious but unfazed by being called 'young man.' In fairness, everyone was young compared to Aethelred.

I followed Aethelred to the back of the house, weaving through narrow hallways until we reached a little kitchen at the back.

He turned to me, blue eyes glinting. "You haven't told the Seelie King that you must kill him to stop your mother from destroying his kingdom."

"So that part is true?"

"I'm afraid it may be."

Damn it. "I'll stop it before it happens. No need to tell."

He frowned. "I hope you're right. But I do think this is an attempt by your mother to draw you to her. You must not go. It is too dangerous. For you, and for the world."

"That's what I'm afraid of."

"Have heart. You may be able to find a way out of this." Aethelred shuffled off to the corner of the kitchen and climbed onto a stool. He reached to the top of the shelf and pulled down a little tin, then fished around inside. After he retrieved something, he returned to me and held out a small golden charm on a chain. "Wear this. It is an amulet that will help strengthen your gift."

I took it and clasped it around my neck. "Thank you."

He nodded. "My mother gave it to me over a century ago. Now it will help you. Wear it to the Circle of Night. Clear your mind and focus on your connection with this problem. The answer may well come to you."

"I hope it does." I looked back toward the main living room where Tarron waited. "Because I really hate the future I'm seeing right now."

He squeezed my arm. "Fix it, then we'll take our walk on the beach."

I smiled at him, though I knew it didn't reach my eyes. "Deal."

I just hoped I wouldn't be grieving the loss of Tarron by my own hand by then.

An hour before dawn in Scotland, we met our backup on Factory Row. It was nine p.m. here, and more people were filing into P & P for a night out on the town.

Aeri, Tarron, and I arrived via my transport power to find the three FireSouls ready and waiting for us on the sidewalk outside of their shop. Cass, Del, and Nix were all incredible fighters with some serious magic. The three were best friends, though they acted more like sisters.

"We're waiting for Claire," Del said. She was dressed entirely in her usual black leather, a perfect match for her midnight hair. Bright blue eyes glinted in the light of the street lamp as she met my gaze. "She was worried about you, and when we mentioned we were helping with a bit of backup, she wanted to join."

"Always handy to have a fire mage around." Nix grinned. She was a skilled conjurer and known for her goofy cartoon T-shirts. Today's was a cat playing the piano. In a sense, it was as much of a disguise as my Elvira look. Enemies rarely expected the pretty girl in the cat T-shirt to be able to kick their asses without breaking a sweat.

She genuinely liked the goofy shirts, just like I loved my Elvira dress.

Weirdo. I loved her, but she was a weirdo. I was my own flavor of weirdo, though, so it made sense.

"Here she comes." Cass nodded down the street, her red hair swinging.

I turned to see Claire hurrying out of P & P, dressed in her fighting leathers again. Her dark hair was pulled back in a ponytail, and a smudge of white flour decorated her cheek.

She grinned when she spotted me. "Connor wanted to come, but we decided it was more important for him to keep looking for an antidote to that potion. We've called in backup at the bar, and he's been in his workshop since you came by."

"Thank you. So much. Really." It was good to have friends. Especially in situations like this.

"Let's go," Tarron said. "Dawn will be here soon, and if we decide we want to enter the Unseelie kingdom, we'll need to do it then."

My friends shot us a confused look.

"The Circle of Night only opens at dawn and dusk," I clarified.

Together, we transported directly to the base of Mount Schiehallion. A chilly breeze swept through the valley, and I turned to look for the noble stags that had helped us reach the peak last time. They'd known just how to dodge the booby traps that were buried beneath the mountain soil, keeping us from being blown up.

I explained the drill to the team while Tarron conjured a massive cart full of rowan berries, the stags' preferred treat.

As before, they came out, somehow knowing exactly how many rides we'd need. Each of the seven was huge and beautiful, with a gleaming coat and an unmistakable aura of magic. A beautiful pale one with enormous horns stooped in front of me and knelt. I mounted him—a bit more easily this time, thank Fates—and our group of seven started up the mountain.

We went single file, Tarron's stag taking the lead as moonlight gleamed on us. Night creatures rustled in the heather, and the stags dodged the prickly gorse that grew on the hillside. Oddly enough, there were far fewer booby traps. Before, the stags had had to dart and dodge to keep us all from being blown to smithereens.

This time, we went almost straight up with no issue. Hell, we probably could have walked ourselves.

My heartbeat picked up the pace, nerves tightening my muscles. I looked at Tarron. "This is a bad sign."

"They're probably waiting for us."

I had to agree with him. My mother was smart. She'd know we were coming for her. She could possibly see our moves before we made them, considering I got my gift of premonition from her.

"Get ready, guys," I murmured. "Something is definitely waiting for us."

As we neared the top, we spread out, approaching the stone circle from multiple angles. The moon had not yet set, and it illuminated the tall standing stones so they glowed nearly silver. The sun would be to the horizon soon, and the morning would turn gray.

Heightened awareness made me edgy. I drew in a deep breath, catching the scent of dark magic. Old garbage, rotten fish, burning tires. But no putrid night lilies or brimstone.

"She's not here," I murmured.

"She'd make her minions stand guard," Tarron said. "But she could show at any moment."

I searched the standing stones for any figures, but the tall pillars of rock cast deep shadows. The Unseelie were definitely here, but they were good at sticking to the darkness.

My stomach pitched as we neared. We were about twenty yards from the statues, so I leapt off my stag and patted his neck. "Thanks, pal. You should get out of here."

I didn't want him getting hurt.

He turned and loped down the hillside.

My friends followed suit, and we approached slowly.

I drew a shield from the ether and crept closer.

Wings.

I was still getting used to them. Quickly, I called them from my back, grateful for the practice that made it so much more fluid and easy. Next to me, Tarron's wings flared wide.

Burn appeared next to Tarron, walking alongside the big Fae. He pressed his thorny side against Tarron's thigh, but the king didn't even flinch. I felt the slightest pulse of Tarron's magic, and saw something appear in his hand. He handed it to Burn, who gobbled it up.

My brows rose.

As if sensing my gaze, Tarron looked over. I glanced away, determined to focus on the task.

Aeri drew her mace from the ether, casually swinging the chain so the spiked ball was ready to go. Del adopted her phantom form, turning a pale transparent blue.

Nothing could hurt her when she was like this, but she'd have to turn corporeal for her sword to make contact with her enemy.

Claire called upon a fireball and tossed it lazily in her hand, while Nix drew a bow and arrow. We shared a love of that particular weapon. Cass just kept walking, not bothering with a weapon. She had an arsenal of skills, and knowing her, she'd wait until the last moment to pull one out.

My heart was already thundering in my ears when the first Unseelie launched an attack. It came with a thunderous boom that shook my bones.

4

When they attacked, I didn't see them coming. But there was no missing the enormous blast of flame that shot from the stone circle. It headed right for my friends, never coming anywhere close to me.

Almost as if the Unseelie were under orders not to kill me.

Cass threw out her hand, creating a massive blast of water. It hurtled toward the flame, colliding in midair and sending up a billowing cloud of steam.

"She has powers like mine," Tarron murmured.

"Cass is a mirror mage." I'd always quite envied her ability to replicate the magical gift of any nearby supernatural. I squinted at a dark shadow, then drew a potion bomb from my bag in the ether and hurled it at the figure.

The Unseelie dodged, barely avoiding my bomb. I wished for my bow and arrow, but as long as the Unseelie were trying to hit me with a mind control potion, I needed to be carrying my shield.

Tarron launched himself into the air, flying toward the circle with deadly grace. His wings gleamed like silver lightning when he dived for an Unseelie, his blade at the ready.

The rest of the Fae sprinted toward us, an evil horde with ghostly pale skin and midnight hair. Some took to the air, and I launched myself upward, drawing a sword as I flew toward the closest one.

Below me, Del hacked at an opponent with her steel, making him howl and burn. Aeri swung her mace in a deadly dance, crushing the skull of a Fae who dived for her. Cass and Claire hurled firebombs with deadly precision, while Nix took out the enemy with steel-tipped arrows.

In the air, I collided with the Fae closest to me in a clash of steel, blocking with my shield as he attacked. His midnight black eyes glinted with ferocity. Quickly, I landed a blow to his arm, making black blood well.

His blade slammed into my shield, sending tremors up my arm. I gripped the shield tight and struck again, managing to deliver a killing blow to his neck. His eyes widened as he gripped the cut and tumbled from the air, wings flapping helplessly.

I whirled, searching for another attacker.

Just in time, I spotted a blast of flame headed right toward me. I deflected it with my shield and raced for my attacker, a slender woman with a flowing mane of midnight hair. She drew a long silver sword, and we collided, blades smashing together. She was more skilled than the other Fae, and she swiped my thigh with her blade, leaving a long, burning cut.

I winced and pulled back, then hurtled toward her, smashing my shield into hers. I wasn't as graceful in the air as a full-blooded Fae, but that didn't mean I couldn't beat the shit out of them. The force of my blow made her tumble backward in the air, and I pressed my advantage, slashing her in the side with my sword. The blade cut deep, and she howled.

I struck again, finding an opening and stabbing her through the shoulder. Weakened, she dropped her sword and flew backward.

Right into one of Cass's fireballs.

Howling, she took off into the sky, blazing like a torch.

I spun, searching for more threats.

Tarron was fighting three Fae at once, his blade moving so fast and so powerfully that it was just a blur. Black blood flew in great arcs as he landed his hits.

Shouts and blasts of magic sounded from all around as my friends battled the Unseelie.

"We've got this!" Aeri shouted. "Do your thing!"

She was right. Every enemy was occupied, and if they came for me, my friends would have my back. I needed to try to use my power before reinforcements came.

I flew toward the center of the stone circle that was now illuminated with the pale gray light of dawn. Thirteen tall pillars of rock surrounded a large flat stone in the middle. It was decorated with incredible carvings, thousands of lines twisting and turning around each other like a beautiful, complicated knot.

If I fed it a bit of my black Unseelie blood, it would open and permit me access to the Unseelie realm.

But we weren't doing that now. Not yet.

First, I needed info.

I landed at the edge of the flat stone and knelt.

A second later, Tarron landed next to me. "I've got your back."

"Thanks." I touched the edge of the rock, shutting my eyes and closing my other hand around the charm that Aethelred had given me.

From behind, I could hear something slamming against Tarron's shield. Fireball, maybe.

I shoved the thought away and trusted him to protect me.

Slowly, I drew in a deep breath and focused on the feeling of the stone beneath my fingertips. It was a connection to the Unseelie world—to my mother—and I could feel it deep in my bones. Aethelred's charm buzzed against my palm, some kind of strange seer magic igniting within it. I could almost smell the seer. Old man cologne and brandy.

A vision flared to life in my head.

I was back in the white, cloudy room.

Something tugged at me from the right, and I turned, running toward it.

Through the mist, I spotted the burning Seelie city.

The colorful flames licked around the buildings, and Seelie fought it, spraying it with massive jets of water and magic.

The flames didn't even steam.

The Fae shot more water at it. More and more, until it was a deluge that should have drowned out the fire.

The blaze kept roaring.

No amount of water could douse this enchanted fire.

I ran toward it, trying to figure out what the hell was going on. I got close enough to the inferno that I could hear the Seelie shouting.

"It's Eternal Flame!" shouted a pale-haired woman, her eyes red from the smoke.

"But that's a myth!" shouted a man next to her.

"Look at it, you imbecile! It's there in front of us, the Eternal Flame that never dies."

"What the hell is that?" I screamed.

The Fae didn't answer. No matter how real they looked, they weren't actually there.

I spun, looking for more clues.

There had to be something. Anything.

I spotted another shadow in the distance, so I ran for it, sprinting through the clouds of white fog.

Truth.

It pulled at me.

I stumbled upon my mother, holding a glowing orange crystal. Magic radiated from it, heat and flame. A crazed glow lit her eyes.

I reached for her, desperate to grab the crystal from her hand. It was the source of the flames. *I had to get it.*

Something pulled at me, dragging at my hand. Shocked, I tried to yank it back.

It didn't work.

The force pulled on me, yanking me out of the vision and back into the real world. I got the briefest flash of a pale dawn sky, a stone circle, and battle all around.

Then the portal leading into the Unseelie kingdom pulled at me, yanking me in. I felt a strong hand grip my ankle, trying to pull me back. Tarron.

But the ether tugged harder, pulled me through space. My stomach lurched as I tumbled, finally crashing onto the grass in the middle of a dark grove.

Heart thundering, I staggered upright. Tarron joined me.

We stood in the dark forest in the Unseelie kingdom, right at the portal that entered their world.

"You were pulled in." Tarron spun in a circle, shield and sword raised.

"Shit. We've been abducted." I called upon my shield, going back to back with him.

None too soon.

A dozen Unseelie charged out from behind the cover of the trees, clearly waiting for us. I couldn't smell my mother's dark magic, but she'd be here soon if she wasn't already hiding somewhere.

The Unseelie's eyes glowed with a strange, sycophantic

light. It reminded me of the Unseelie minion who'd stood by my mother's side when I'd seen her last.

There was something strange about that light. Could it be her influence acting through them, forcing them to do her will?

It didn't make sense that they'd all be evil. I knew they weren't. I'd seen the normalcy of parts of their city when I'd visited last. Sensed it in them. They were more likely to go to the dark side, but that didn't mean they all chose to.

"Get to the portal." I backed toward it, shoving Tarron.

He moved swiftly, reaching it as the Unseelie began to hurl fire and ice. They were as adept with nature magic as the Seelie.

"The portal is blocked," Tarron said.

There was no time left to argue.

Burn appeared next to me, hackles raised and growling.

I spun to face the oncoming attackers, spotting the blast of energy as it hurtled at us. It was just a glimmer, and I caught it too late to brace myself.

The energy slammed into me, Tarron, and Burn. Pain exploded within me, and we were hurled up into the air. Panic flashed as I flew, then I crashed to the ground with a hard thud. Agony spread from my back.

Ears ringing, I stared up into the canopy above. Dark leaves quivered against an even darker sky, and I blinked.

For the briefest moment, my mind was entirely blank.

Then it all came back.

I staggered upright as fast as I could. I'd flown far

enough away from the battle that I had a few seconds to recover. My muscles felt like jelly and my entire body was a mass of pain. I was a good twenty feet from Tarron, who was already fighting off two Unseelie attackers. He was so pale he was almost transparent, and his movements were stiff. That hit had nearly killed him, too. The three of us had taken the brunt of it, distributing the force and probably saving our lives.

Despite his injuries, the Unseelie were no match for Tarron. He moved with such deadly power and grace that they were dead within seconds. Two more piled onto him, but he cut them down as well, his sword slicing them right through the middle. I'd never seen a fighter like him.

He loomed over an Unseelie who'd fallen to the ground, sword raised over the smaller Fae. The figure scrambled back, fear flashing on his face. For the briefest moment, the sycophantic light faded from the Unseelie's eyes. He looked around, frantic and shocked.

Like he was surprised to be there.

Holy fates.

Maybe that Unseelie really *was* under the influence of my mother. And now—somehow—her magic had faded from his mind.

I'd suspected it, but seeing it play out in front of my eyes made it so obvious.

The Unseelie raised his hands. "No, please."

I could just barely hear his words as he begged for his life.

I nearly lunged for them, determined to stop Tarron

from killing the smaller Fae.

But Tarron's blade hesitated.

He could see what I did.

Despite his rage with the Unseelie for what they'd done to his kingdom and his brother, he stopped.

The Unseelie crawled away. Another came at Tarron from behind, his eyes bright with the light of my mother's influence.

"Tarron!" I shouted.

The king turned and spotted his attacker. Swift as a wraith, he raised his sword and cut down the Unseelie who lunged for his throat, obsidian blade gleaming in the light.

Fates, this sucked. Some of these Fae were genuinely against us, but others probably weren't. It didn't matter when they were trying to kill us, though, and I was probably cutting down those who didn't deserve to die.

To Tarron's right, Burn leapt at the throat of a third Unseelie. The wolf looked faster and stronger—twice as big.

Oh right. Tarron had once told me how an attack could make the Thorn Wolf grow stronger temporarily. He was the perfect fighting machine, and the massive attack from the Fae with the energy blast had given him a real hit of power. He tore through the Unseelie with a speed and rage that paralleled Tarron's.

"Fight your way back to the portal!" I shouted.

We had to try again. There had to be a way through.

I looked behind me, making sure no attack was coming, then crouched behind my shield and ran. I didn't want to fly—that would give them one more angle to hit me from.

As I sprinted, I drew a potion bomb from the ether. I was really plowing through them today, and I wished that the stock Aeri and I had made hadn't been destroyed in the attack on our home.

An Unseelie lunged out from behind a tree, raising a flaming hand. His eyes gleamed with a crazed light, and I threw my potion bomb, aiming for his chest. It slammed right into him.

Whatever tug I felt in my conscience for hitting someone who might be under the influence of my mother's magic, I ignored it. They would kill me as long as her power ran through them, and I couldn't afford to die.

Not when the Seelie kingdom might burn.

Another sprinted toward me, sword raised. It glinted silver in the moonlight, and the Fae's wide eyes met mine. The manic light glowed within them.

I drew a steel sword from the ether and charged, my blade clashing with his. With our swords locked at the hilt, I lunged toward him, kneeing him in the balls. He choked and doubled over. I yanked my sword free and plunged it through his gut, then kicked him away.

Panting, I swung around, searching for the big threat—the blast of magic that had thrown the three of us into the air like piñata pieces.

In the distance, I spotted a huge Fae, far taller and broader than any I'd ever seen. The magic that seethed around him made the air shimmer.

That had to be the guy who'd thrown the massive, murderous energy blast.

And I doubted he needed my mother's magic to sway him to do bad things. I could smell his dark magic from where I stood.

He raised his hand, which was nearly impossible to see because of the way the air waved around it and distorted the image.

My heart jumped into my throat. I *so* did not want to get hit again. Somehow, I knew he'd been pulling his punches the first time.

"Tarron!" I shouted.

He looked over, then cursed, diving to the side as the giant threw his magic at him. The blast was too big.

Tarron wouldn't make it.

A second hit like the first could kill him.

I lunged in front of him, bracing myself for the hit.

Please let this work.

My heartbeat thundered as the magic shot toward me. I called upon my new power to reflect the magic back at the sender. Cold sweat broke out on my brow right before the blast plowed into me. Then it hit.

I went blind with the pain and slammed backward into the ground.

Using this power had never hurt so bad.

"Mari!" Tarron's agonized shout sounded from behind me.

I tried to rise, but I couldn't.

Had my power even worked?

Strong arms pulled me up, cradling me close. Through bleary vision, I saw the collapsed form of the powerful Fae who had attacked us.

My power *had* worked.

Except it might have broken me, too.

"Get to the portal," I croaked.

"It's closed."

"Have...an idea."

The Unseelie closed in, and Burn leapt in front of us. The huge wolf crouched low and growled, his thorny hide shooting spiked bullets at the oncoming attackers. The deadly thorns flew through the air, piercing the Unseelie like daggers.

The scent of putrid night lilies and brimstone rolled toward us.

I gasped. "She's coming."

"We're in no state to take her out now."

"You and Burn could take her." But he'd have to drop me to do it, and the Unseelie would be on me in an instant. I still couldn't move my limbs. There'd be no fighting back.

Tarron ignored my words and sprinted toward the portal, holding me as if I were made of crystal.

As we neared it, I sliced my finger with my sharp thumbnail.

"We needed blood to get in the first time." My voice was weak, and he leaned closer to hear. "Maybe Unseelie blood will help us get out."

I stuck my hand into the shimmering air that marked the exit from this realm, and magic shivered up my arm.

My blood turned cool on my fingertip, then magic sparked from the gleaming surface of the portal.

"Go!" I shouted.

Tarron lunged into the portal.

I peered back at Burn. "Get out of here!"

The Thorn Wolf disappeared in an instant. Beyond him, the bodies of a dozen Unseelie lay like giant pincushions. My mother appeared in the distance, gliding through the trees with eerie grace.

The ether sucked us in and swept us through space. My stomach lurched and my limbs ached.

We appeared back in Scotland, surrounded by the thirteen towering stones of the Circle of Night.

My friends crowded near, all white-faced and big-eyed.

"You're back!" Aeri rushed forward.

"We need to go," Tarron said.

"No!" I grabbed his arm. "If she comes, we can take her. The six of you are strong enough."

It would kill me to sit out the fight, but I knew that if Tarron put me down, I'd be a puddle of jello with all the movement of a slug.

But they could totally take her.

"We can't risk it." Tarron gave everyone a look. "Can one of you transport and get the others out of here?"

"We're covered," Cass said.

"No!" I squeezed his arm tighter.

He didn't listen. He called upon his transport power—which he used rarely, I realized—and disappeared.

Once again, the ether sucked us in.

5

We appeared in his quarters, high in the king's tower in the middle of the Seelie Court.

"Why did you do that?" I demanded. "Do you know how powerful they are? The FireSouls could have taken out my mother if she'd come through the portal."

"You can't even walk." A thunderous expression crossed his face. "I'm not starting a fight with an extremely powerful Fae who has mind control powers while you can't protect yourself."

"That's—"

My brain did a record scratch.

Damn it.

That was really caring.

I frowned up at him, confused. "What about your brother? Your vengeance? We almost had her."

"No, we didn't. And we'll worry about that later." He stalked toward the bed.

I blinked. All he cared about was vengeance for his brother. Right?

"Why the hell did you jump in front of me like that?" His brow was lowered, his eyes angry. "You could have died."

"You would have died. Only my power protected me."

"Don't ever do that again."

"What, save your life?"

"Risk yours for mine." He looked like he wanted to shake me but didn't dare. "I'm not worth it."

He cared. I swallowed hard and looked away, uncertain how to process that.

Or the fact that I'd jumped in front of him.

I didn't risk my life for a lot of people.

But I'd done it for him.

Of course you did it for him, idiot.

I looked around his quarters. "Why are we here?"

"It's safer."

"My place is fine."

"What don't you understand about the fact that I'd do anything to protect you?"

"Wow. Um, this is not expected."

"You're kidding, right? I may be angry about your lies and trust you as far as I can throw you, but I will *always* protect you."

"You're compelled to do it. Because I'm your *Mograh*."

"Because I *want* to do it." His tone was so fierce that I didn't argue, but when he put me on the bed, it felt like he was laying down his most precious possession.

Even so, I winced. It felt like thousands of needles were stabbing me all over my body. Like when your leg goes asleep, but everywhere.

"Now shut up." His tone was sharp.

I scowled at him.

Until he pressed his hands to my shoulders and began to feed his healing energy into me. His brow was furrowed with concern and his mouth went tight with worry.

"You're worried about me," I breathed.

He shot me a look that suggested I was an idiot, then said gruffly, "Of course I am. Now lie still."

His healing power flowed through me, taking away the agony that pervaded every inch of my body. As the pain faded, my head cleared.

Tarron was really worried about me. And frustrated by it.

I could feel it.

The healing power created a connection between us, and the desire to protect me roared through him.

It warmed something inside me—something primal.

Yet I was fated to kill him.

I squeezed my eyes shut, trying to drive out the memory of the premonition.

With my eyes closed, my other senses heightened. I couldn't help but focus on the warmth of his hands. The sound of his breathing. The scent of his skin.

Heat shot through me.

Desire.

With the pain gone, all I could think about was his touch.

All I *wanted* to think about was his touch. Because everything else was a disaster. And this wasn't.

Far from it.

It felt like the most natural thing in the world. Like we were being pushed together in the best way possible.

The energy in the air changed. It was as if he could sense the desire that gripped me. His touch on my shoulders tightened possessively, and I moaned.

"Mari." My name sounded torn from his throat, his voice tortured.

I opened my eyes and caught a look of such desire on his face that it made me shiver.

Despite everything, I wanted him.

He swept me into his arms, and a low groan rumbled from his throat as his mouth crashed down on mine. Heat exploded through me as his lips moved expertly on my own.

He nipped and laved, and I plunged my hands into his hair, holding him close. His scent wrapped around me, a crisp autumn day along with the more intimate smell of his skin. His soap.

I pressed every inch of my body against him, running my hands down his neck and along the muscles of his shoulders and arms.

He cupped my head in one huge hand and cradled me against him with the other, curved protectively over me in the bed. As if he'd never let anyone get to me.

"We shouldn't." His voice sounded ragged as he laid me back on the bed, his actions belying his words.

"I don't care." I reached for him, pulling him down.

His weight pressed me to the mattress, his harder angles aligning perfectly with the dips and curves of my body. Pleasure shot through me, from my center to every inch of my extremities. He moved against me in the most perfect rhythm, and I shuddered.

I couldn't resist him any longer.

This thing had been pulling at us forever, fate determined to push us together.

Fate...

Was that the only reason we were doing this?

My comms charm blared, pulling me from the moment. Tarron groaned, a sound of such tortured frustration that something tugged inside me.

Aeri's voice blasted out of my comms charm. "I'm at the damned entrance to this stupid Fae realm, and I can't get in! Mari, you better be there!"

I flopped back on the bed and groaned.

Tarron pulled away from me, dragging a hand through his hair. His eyes had turned fully black and his horns had appeared. Fangs glinted white against his lips. "I'll take care of it."

I touched my comms charm. "Tarron is sending someone to you."

"Good," Aeri snapped.

Tarron rose, lifting himself off me and climbing off the bed to stride to the other side of the room.

While he called on someone to get Aeri from Kilmartin, I drew in a shuddery breath and sat up. My injuries were gone, and I felt fine. More than fine, actually, if I ignored the thwarted desire still racing through my veins.

"We need to stop doing that," I said, even as I knew it wouldn't happen.

"Agreed." He turned to me, eyes flashing. The signs of his arousal were gone—horns disappeared and fangs retracted—but darkness still gleamed in his eyes. "How do you propose we stop?"

"Chastity belt?"

He raised a brow.

"For you, not me." I grinned.

He cracked a smile.

A knock sounded at the door.

He moved to answer, and I sagged backward. Good timing. Definitely good timing.

While he answered, I turned and pressed my hands to my hot cheeks. I needed to get myself under control. This was ridiculous.

I popped a butterscotch candy into my mouth and sucked hard, but it did nothing to distract me.

"Here, eat." His voice sounded from behind.

I whirled around to see him carrying a tray laden with food toward a table near the wall.

"I'm good." I stuck out my tongue to show him the candy sitting there.

His eyes flickered with heat. After the briefest hesitation, he spoke. "That doesn't count. Eat real food."

"You don't have to take care of me, you know."

"Maybe I want to." With that, he turned away and laid out the food.

Holy fates, he was just going to drop that bomb and pretend he'd never said an insane thing like that?

I walked up to him, curious.

Before I reached him, there was another knock on the door. He left to open it, and I grabbed a sandwich from the tray. There was a bowl of fruit, and none of it looked like the Fae fruit that would make me feel compelled to stay here forever.

Aeri entered behind Tarron.

"Well, did you learn what you needed to?" she asked.

Tarron looked at me like he'd been wondering the same thing all along and was confused as to why I hadn't mentioned it.

I wanted to remind him that he'd been kissing my face off the whole time.

I swallowed the bite of sandwich. "Sort of. I know that she's after the Eternal Flame. And it's something important." I met Tarron's gaze. "Your people seemed to know something about it in the vision I had."

He nodded. "Aye, that's possible. I've heard it mentioned before."

"Well, my mother is after it, and she'll use it to destroy your kingdom. From within."

He nodded. "We need to see how the preparations are coming for the upcoming attack."

"*Potential* upcoming attack." I *would* stop this. Though I was getting more worried about that. The more time passed, the more likely it seemed that it might happen.

In which case, I really needed to tell Tarron about my vision of his death.

He nodded. "Potential attack. We'll meet with the Court Guard, make sure everything is going according to plan, then we'll see what we can find out about the Eternal Flame from Arrowen the Seer."

"Then we'll hunt down my mother and kill her." Saying the words turned my stomach.

It was necessary, but hell, it sucked.

Why was this my life?

It had been going so smoothly before.

Aeri reached for my hand and squeezed, as if she could read my thoughts. She didn't remember her mother, and right now, I was envious. Far better for her to be a mystery than a murderer.

Tarron led the way through the castle, and Aeri and I stuck a few feet back, whispering about the Fae we saw and the fantastic architecture. The whole place still blew my mind. The sheer size and graceful elegance of it was astounding. I preferred my Gothic townhouse in Darklane, but the wide hallways and towering ceilings of Tarron's castle followed a close second.

It lacked the musty coldness of most castles I'd been to, probably a combination of the fact that it was currently occupied and Fae sensibilities. Because the realm was protected and hidden—for the most part—the castle was more like a fabulous residence than a stronghold. Enormous windows dotted the hallways, each of them glassless to allow a lovely breeze to flow through. Diaphanous curtains floated on the wind. The air smelled fresh—of flowers and cool water.

"They must never have bad weather," Aeri muttered.

"I think they control it somehow. The Fae are great with nature magic."

"Good point."

I looked out the window, spying the rolling hills of the Seelie kingdom, each speckled with the glowing lights of houses. The Unseelie realm had been beautiful in its own way, too. A darker half of the same coin.

Finally, we reached the war room.

Tarron led the way into the long, rectangular space that was full of waiting Fae. As soon as they spotted him, they surged to their feet, eyes alert. Each one—except for the old seer Arrowen—wore a uniform of gold and red that was perfectly pressed. Arrowen's silver dress sparkled like stars. It really looked quite fab on her. Maybe I should try silver.

In unison, they all bowed low. The sense of respect on the air was so strong that I thought I could grab it and hold it. I'd missed this bit when I'd come to the war room last, because Tarron had already been here.

"You may rise." Tarron stalked toward the table that was covered with a massive three-dimensional model.

The Fae all straightened, looking at him with varying shades of respect or deep fear. No matter what, this group would follow his orders to the death—that was obvious. As for the respect or fear that glinted on their faces, I had a feeling it had to do with whether or not they knew the truth about his brother's death and Tarron's ascension to the throne.

I wished they knew the truth about him. The self-sacrifice astounded me.

But that was exactly what Tarron didn't want.

So I kept my mouth shut.

Luna strode forward, her blue hair tied up in a complicated braid and her pink eyes keen. I hadn't seen much of Tarron's right-hand Fae since the competition where we'd first met, but from the tired look in her eyes, she'd been hard at work.

Luna met Tarron at the edge of the table. "We've been shoring up the entrances to the realm and the weak spots in the ether."

There was curiosity in her voice. Tarron must not have told them *why*.

I joined them at the table, Aeri at my side. A closer inspection revealed that this was a three-dimensional map of the entire kingdom. Certain parts at the edge were marked with blue crystal.

"What are the crystals?" I asked.

"Weak spots in the ether or entrances to our realm." Luna met me with an assessing gaze. "Sometimes both."

"Why are there weak spots?"

Luna shrugged. "It's the nature of the ether. It's how we built the portals to our realm, so no complaints from us." She looked at Tarron. "Until now. What's the deal?"

"The Queen of the Unseelie—the same one who launched the attack on the King's Grove—is planning to invade with Eternal Flame."

A series of low gasps sounded throughout the room.

Luna paled. "That can't be right."

"I'm afraid so."

"She'll likely bring demons," I said. "She hires them as mercenaries. Her forces could be impressive."

Another guard stepped up, this one tall and pale, with brilliant blue eyes and magic that smelled of dew and dawn. "We can't possibly guard all the entrances against a Fae queen with Eternal Flame."

"You're going to have to." Tarron's voice was cold, brooking no argument.

"We'll need backup," Luna said.

Tarron nodded sharply. "We'll find it."

"I can help with that," Aeri said. "We have friends who will help."

Again, I was grateful for my years in Magic's Bend. I hadn't set out to make friends who would have my back, but somehow I'd managed it.

Arrowen leaned forward. The seer was ancient, though she possessed a timeless beauty. Her white hair was a halo around her head. Sharp blue eyes assessed the map and then Tarron. "Does the Unseelie Queen have the flame yet?"

"We assume not," Tarron said. "Or we'd already be on fire."

I bit back a huff of laughter.

That shouldn't be funny.

But it was.

Arrowen even gave a wry, dark chuckle.

I stood by, listening as Tarron discussed the various entrances to the Seelie kingdom with his guard. They debated which soldiers to place where, how long it would take reinforcements to move from portal to portal, and which allies could be called upon from the outside world.

They were preparing like this would happen—like the queen would make it into the realm.

If she did, it would only end with their king's death.

I shivered and shoved the thought aside.

"If the dark queen enters the realm, it will be nearly impossible to stop her," Arrowen said. "Eternal Flame takes almost nothing to ignite. All she'll have to do is throw it."

Tarron nodded, face drawn. "We'll call on mages to help us lock the entrances more tightly."

It was no guarantee. Even I knew that.

But it was all we could do.

"Nothing can douse an Eternal Flame?" Aeri asked.

"Nothing that we know of," Arrowen said.

Except for Tarron's death, though that made no sense to me.

"We need to stop her before she gets here," Luna said.

"Agreed." Tarron nodded. "Mari and I will be focusing

on that."

I appreciated that he used the name Mari, which is what I'd used in the tournament. I liked that he remembered that was the name I'd chosen to go by in his realm.

"Could you infiltrate her realm to take her out?" asked the tall, pale Fae guard who'd spoken earlier.

Tarron shook his head. "When we entered just an hour ago, there were so many guards that we would never make it to her."

"Not to mention, I don't think they were acting of their own accord," I said.

Arrowen frowned. "What do you mean?"

"I believe that my mother's mind control magic has influenced some of the Unseelie to act in her stead. Otherwise, they might not."

"Your mother?" Luna's brows rose.

There were murmurs from around the room.

The Fae hadn't realized that she was my mother, but now that Tarron knew, I had no reason to keep it a secret. I was used to people whispering about me, and I needed to try to be as honest as I could.

"Precisely." I met Luna's eyes, my own gaze hard. "And I want to stop her as much as you do."

"Then we should invade their realm," said the pale guard. "With more of our warriors. Bring the fight to them."

"It would kill too many," I said. "Seelie and Unseelie both. The Unseelie aren't all evil. Their magic is dark, but that doesn't make them explicitly evil." *I* wasn't evil.

"Who cares about the Unseelie?" Disdain sounded in his voice.

I opened my mouth to retort, but Tarron beat me to it.

"Enough." He slashed his hand through the air, his voice cracking like a whip. "We will attempt to stop the queen without invading her realm. It's not worth the loss of life. *On both sides.*"

I warmed slightly. He'd spared the young Unseelie's life in our most recent fight, so he clearly was seeing the same thing I was.

"Why is she coming here?" Luna asked. "Her first invasion seemed designed to sway us to her side. But this... It's wholesale destruction. Murder."

"She was initially after this realm to expand her empire." My voice was cold. "She's accepted we'll stop her no matter what. Now, she wants to destroy this place."

A low grumbling sounded from the Seelie who stood away from the table. I could hear whispers of *her mother.*

Tarron's cold voice struck. "Enough. Or I will evict you from the court forever."

The ruthlessness in his tone made me shiver.

I'd forgotten that side of him. Almost. The cold and ruthless king. I'd seen it initially, before we'd gotten to know each other.

But it was part of him.

Tarron wrapped up the rest of the planning meeting quickly. Finally, the Court Guard departed, moving swiftly to the door to continue their work. Only Arrowen stayed.

"As for the next part of our plan," Tarron said. "We must seek the Eternal Flame."

I looked at Arrowen. "Do you know anything about it?"

It was a myth I was vaguely familiar with, but I'd never had reason to know it before.

"The Eternal Flame is as ancient as magic itself," Arrowen said. The old seer leaned forward, her face alight with power and her dress a glittering silver.

Her tone was hushed with awe when she continued. "It has been guarded by the goddesses of fire since time immemorial."

"Where is it located?" I asked.

"No one knows," Arrowen said.

"Seriously? *No one?*" I frowned.

"Only the Guardians of the Eternal Flame know where the flame is located," Arrowen said. "They live in an ever-changing place, nearly impossible to find."

"Just our luck." I frowned. "So they guard the fire. If we find them, we find the flame."

"Not quite," Arrowen said. "The flame will be relatively close to them, but they don't guard it personally. It's too unpleasant. Hot as hell and the magic that guards it is vicious. The goddesses control that magic and decide where the flame will live, but they do not stay with the flame itself."

"The flame itself moves?" Tarron asked.

"Indeed. There are many locations that have been the home of the Eternal Flame, all of them deadly. You must find the Guardians and ask where the flame is located."

"Why couldn't we just try to find the flame?" Aeri said.

"Only the goddesses can give you permission to access it, and even then, it will be a deadly journey. Without them, you will search forever, fruitlessly."

"Which means that my mother must go to them first."

Arrowen inclined her head. "Most likely."

"We need to beat her there, then lay in wait." Tarron turned his gaze to me. "You don't know when this attack will happen, do you?"

"No. I couldn't see that. But it felt very soon." It might have been my fear of his death that made it feel that way, but I swore it was breathing down my neck.

Tarron turned to Arrowen. "Can you see when? Or where it will happen?"

"I'll try."

I stood, breath held, as Arrowen closed her eyes and her magic flared on the air.

Tension tightened the air in the room as we all waited.

Finally, she opened her eyes. Before she even spoke, I knew the answer.

"I could not see when or where."

"Damn it." If she was unable to see the location of the goddess of the Eternal Flame, we had no leads.

"Who are they?" Tarron asked. "Which goddesses?"

"Hestia, Vesta, Brigid, and Arinitti." Arrowen frowned. "Though they may change with time, with other goddesses from different pantheons coming in to do their time guarding the flame."

"These are the four you know of, so we'll look for

them." I knew three of the names. Hestia was Greek, Vesta Roman, and Brigid Celtic. "But who is Arinitti?"

"Hittite sun goddess of the city Arinna."

"Hittite?" Aeri asked. "The ancient culture that once lived in Turkey?"

"The very same." Arrowen nodded. "Over three thousand years ago."

Okay. That gave us something to work with.

I looked between Tarron and Aeri. "I'll try my power. See if I can see something."

"I'll help," Tarron said.

"Thanks." He'd helped me practice my wings before, and his magic had made me stronger. Right now, we needed all the advantage we could get. "If I'm going to do this, it would help to have something to jumpstart my gift." I looked around the room, spotting the big hearth. The weather was too temperate for a fire to be burning, but we could light one. "I'm probably closest to Brigid. She's Irish, but she's still a Celtic Goddess and we Unseelie are Celtic. And the Tuath Dé anann respect her."

I'd never met the Irish Fae, but the connection in our blood and species couldn't hurt.

"Do you want a weapon or something?" Aeri asked. "Isn't she the goddess of smithing as well as fire?"

"You read my mind." Like many of the ancient goddesses, Brigid had overseen many aspects of life. Not just flame, but also poetry, arts, and metalworking.

I met Tarron's gaze. "Iron was most common around

the Celts. I'm going to draw an iron blade, if you'll permit it?"

Because the Fae were extra sensitive to iron—way more so than I—it felt polite to ask.

He nodded.

I went to the fire. Tarron grabbed a heavy chair from the table and carried it over in one hand. He set it down in front of the empty hearth, then thrust his hand toward it. His magic swelled on the air, and a fire burst to life, crackling merrily.

"Thanks." I sat in the chair, calling an iron dagger from the ether. I gripped the hilt tight, my skin itching faintly. Maybe it was silly to hold it, but talismans often helped with magic.

I'd do whatever it took to find these damned goddesses in order to stop my mother. Just using this premonition magic—which I'd gotten from her, apparently—made me feel closer to her.

I hated it.

"I'm going to touch your shoulders, all right?" Tarron asked.

I nodded, already anticipating his touch.

Arrowen and Aeri stepped up alongside us as Tarron placed his large hands on my shoulders. Heat raced through me, and my world narrowed to just the place our bodies joined.

I sucked in a deep breath and yanked myself out of the trance.

Now was *so* not the time.

6

The flames flickered and danced in front of me. The iron burned. I focused on those things, shuddering slightly as Tarron fed his magic into my soul.

His power flowed through my veins, igniting my own. It was impossible not to feel a connection with him. Our fated mate bond, combined with sharing our magic, made me feel like we were attached on a soul-deep level.

I drew in an unsteady breath. His ability was spectacular. There was nothing he couldn't accomplish with this.

And I could *feel* him. Who he was. The goodness in him. The ruthlessness. He'd sacrificed himself for his people when he'd taken on the role of king.

He'd do it again if he had to.

I could feel it.

And I was desperate to stop it. The future that barreled down on us was unbearable.

I used that desperation, calling up every bit of my magic.

It burst to life inside me, the power swelling up through my chest and filling my mind. My vision went black and I stood in the white room. Clouds rolled along the ground around me, filling the space.

Where is Brigid?

I asked the one concrete question that might help me stop all of this from happening.

It took a moment, as if the information were buried deep in the ether. I gripped the blade in my hand tightly, letting the iron burn me as I tried to forge a connection with the Celtic goddess who had Fae connections.

To my left, Burn woofed low in his throat.

I looked down, spotting the Thorn Wolf. He looked into the distance, eyes bright.

"Thanks, pal." I moved in that direction, following the command of the animal who had become my familiar.

Tarron's power stayed with me as I moved through the vision, giving me strength and clearing the clouds away even faster. They dissipated to reveal a beautiful red-haired woman. Her eyes were the same magnificent green as her dress.

"Brigid." Of course she didn't turn to look at me.

She stood on a tall plateau, the sun setting behind her. It burned like fire as it dropped low, casting the plateau in shadows. I searched for details, spotting strange carvings on the massive cliff upon which the plateau sat.

They looked like buildings, carved right into the

stone, halfway up the cliff wall. They were ancient, a place I'd never seen. They looked like Petra, in Jordan. The famous site was a supernatural hot spot. But this was different.

Brigid stood on the plateau above, the sun illuminating her hair. Trees scattered around her, appearing to light on fire from the setting sun. The air smelled of smoke and fire.

I had no idea what this place was.

Panic lit in my chest. This could be so many places in the world. I ran forward, trying to find clues. I spotted ancient ruins. Greek or Roman, maybe. Others that were unfamiliar. They scattered about the landscape below the plateau, the strangest thing I'd ever seen.

But the most distinct thing about the place was the sun that lit it on fire.

It's not enough.

I couldn't find her with just this.

If I couldn't find her, Tarron would die.

Images flashed in my mind. A vision inside a vision.

Me, killing Tarron. Tears pouring down my face. Tarron, tortured. Determined.

Something yanked on my shoulders, pulling me back.

I gasped, my mind torn from the premonition. Choking, I opened my eyes. The first thing I saw was fire.

Panic flared.

Someone swept me up.

Tarron.

I was in Tarron's arms.

Big and strong, he gripped me tight, carrying me away from the fire. My breath heaved.

I was hyperventilating.

I was absolutely losing my shit.

It was unacceptable.

Determined, I drew in a ragged breath, trying to slow my heart rate and calm my mind. Get my act together. "You can put me down."

"Are you sure?" Concern echoed in Tarron's voice.

"Yes."

He set me down on the other side of the room, and I stumbled back, running my hands down the front of my body, trying to straighten my clothes.

"Mari?" Aeri's voice sounded from the other side of the room.

I looked over, trying to compose myself. I *loathed* freaking out and losing my composure in public. It just wasn't me.

"Are you okay?" she asked.

"Fine." My voice *almost* sounded brisk. I'd take it. "I saw some things. Hopefully enough."

"Like what?" Tarron's voice drew my attention to him, and I met his gaze.

The memory of stabbing him flashed in my mind.

I twitched.

Damn it, I was going to get nightmares from this.

I shoved the thought away. I would stop it.

A little voice whispered that I should tell him about it,

but I knew it wouldn't matter. We had to stop the queen. Tarron wouldn't step away because of risk to himself.

"I saw Brigid. She stood on a plateau that was lit with a flaming sun." I described everything I'd seen, searching the eyes of the three people around me, hoping for a glint of recognition.

When I saw it in Arrowen's eyes, I nearly sagged with relief. "You recognize something."

"The flaming planes, topped with a plateau lit by the sun." She nodded. "This is a place, near the Lycian rock-cut tombs. It's famous among our kind, and located in the ancient Anatolia."

"Turkey?"

"The very same. It doesn't surprise me that the Guardians of the Eternal Flame would make that their home."

"What about all the archaeological ruins I saw there? I don't know much about history, but they appeared to be from different cultures. Different kinds of stone were used, different construction."

"Very likely the goddesses' impact. They'd want to be among the familiar. It's more than possible that what you saw acts as a guard for them. Protecting them."

"Humans can't go there, can they?" Aeri asked. "Their archaeologists would freak out if there were true ruins in places there shouldn't be. Cultures sitting next to each other that never interacted."

"Precisely," Arrowen said.

"So just supernaturals. Us included." I looked at Tarron. "When can we leave?"

"Immediately. We should have some potions on hand for energy. In case we cannot sleep."

I nodded. "Good."

We'd have to be careful. One couldn't take too many of those potions without terrible effects. And we'd need to save our magic. The potions wouldn't necessarily restore that the way true rest would.

I looked at Aeri. "Can I speak to you privately?"

Tarron's brows rose, but I said nothing to him.

Aeri nodded, and we left the room, finding a discreet corner of the castle where a statue of a stag rose tall and proud. I tucked myself back behind the statue and pulled her in with me.

Then I did something I rarely did, and never while we were standing close together. I used my power to appear inside her mind. It was one of my oldest magics. The walls could have ears.

Aeri. I need a favor.

She nodded, eyes wide.

I keep seeing that prophecy of me killing Tarron. It won't go away like I hoped it would. Can you try to find out why his magic might stop hers? It must be something about them both being Fae royalty, I think.

"Yes. Of course I'll work on that. I promise. And I'll help find reinforcements for the Unseelie."

I squeezed her hand tight. *Thanks.*

"I'm out of here." She hugged me, then we parted ways.

I watched her walk down the hall, hope and worry tangling in my chest. We'd never failed at something we'd put our mind to.

I hoped now wouldn't be the first time.

∼

Tarron and I reconvened in the war room. Arrowen had left, and the room echoed hollowly.

"You're hiding something," he said.

"No." *Lies.*

He frowned, and decided to ignore me.

"We need to get moving," I said. "It could take a while to find the Guardians."

He gave me a hard look, then nodded. "We'll stop by the potions master and stock up. Then we'll transport directly to Anatolia, near the Lycian tombs that Arrowen mentioned."

I couldn't argue with that plan.

He led me through the castle, down to a huge, airy room where the potions master worked. The Fae within was a slight figure, so pale she was nearly transparent. Her hair was so fine it appeared to float on the air, ethereal and pale. I browsed the supplies as Tarron collected what we needed. I was really quite impressed.

He returned to me. "Ready?"

"Ready."

We left the room, and I called back a quick thanks over my shoulder. The Fae ignored me.

Outside, we each drank one of the potions, which actually tasted good. That was rare.

"Do you want to do the honors?" I asked.

"My transport powers don't work like that," he said.

"What do you mean?"

"I can only transport to my home."

"But you once said you could transport to me."

"Like I said."

He considered me home? "It's part of the fated mate thing, isn't it?"

"Apparently so."

I'd think on that later. I reached out my hand. He took it. As soon as his stronger palm closed around my own, I called upon my transport magic. I envisioned the place I'd seen, imagining the region in southern Turkey where we would appear. I tried to use a bit of my seeker sense as well, hoping to zero in on the goddesses' location.

The ether sucked us in and pulled us through space, spitting us out in the middle of a landscape of pale dirt and small trees. The sun burned high overhead, bright and fierce. It was headed toward the horizon and would eventually set behind an enormous plateau.

"I'm going to try to transport us directly there." I reached for Tarron's hand.

He gripped mine, and I tried to get us closer. The ether resisted.

I dropped his palm. "No surprise."

He studied the landscape in front of us. From here, we

couldn't see any of the ancient ruins I'd seen in my vision, but they'd be here, nestled amongst the trees.

Together, we set off, tension high. There would be protections between us and the Guardians. We'd just have to manage to survive them.

I kept my senses alert as we walked, trying to feel the magic before it struck. When we came upon the first set of ancient ruins, I hesitated.

"Around or through?" Tarron asked.

"Um...through. There might be information within." My seeker sense felt a bit of a tug, and I didn't want to miss any clues or tricks for how to reach the goddesses. You could never tell what you might learn.

We approached the broken-down stone building, and I admired the crumbling architecture. The white stone and columns made it look vaguely Roman or Greek. The ruins were quite well preserved given their age. Most of the places I'd visited or seen pictures of were lacking their roofs, but not here.

We entered the structure on silent feet, passing by strange rooms with pits in the middle.

"Roman baths," Tarron said.

"Ah, of course." I'd have liked to have seen it when it was operational.

All the same, it was almost as if I could feel the ghosts of the past here, and I hurried, wanting to be done with this place. We reached the other side of the building, stepping through the archway that was now missing its door and into the forest beyond. From where I stood, I could see a path that had been trodden down in the dirt. It was faint, but definitely there, leading from the doorway into the thickening forest.

I used my seeker sense, hoping it would pick something up. It tugged in the direction that the path led.

Tarron knelt to study it. "Good idea to go through. We wouldn't have seen this if we'd gone around."

"Are those hoof prints?"

"Yes. From the gait, it looks like they belong to a two-footed beast."

"A Satyr, perhaps?"

"That would be my guess." He stood and started down the path.

I joined his side.

The path was quiet, with just the faintest sparkle of magic in the air.

"I don't feel like we're alone," I murmured, inspecting the empty forest around us.

"I think there's something we're not seeing."

Tension tightened my muscles as we walked. I didn't dare draw a weapon yet—no need to provoke—but my fingers itched to.

Finally, we reached a clearing. A ruined coliseum stood in the middle of it. Not as big as the one in Rome, but impressive nonetheless.

"Head for it?" Tarron asked.

"Yes." I started forward, eyes wary.

We reached the coliseum a few minutes later. I leaned

back to look up at the towering walls. "I think we should enter."

Tarron nodded. We found an entry and made our way through the darkened corridor to the front, where the area opened up into the sunlight. Empty stadium seating encircled a fighting ring, and I swore I could hear the clang of swords and the shouts of viewers.

I leaned toward Tarron and whispered, "Do you hear that?"

He stepped closer. "I do."

"Let's go to the top." I didn't know why I felt drawn there, but I couldn't resist it.

We climbed to the top, and I felt the rush of energy through the ancient stadium. "People are here. We just can't see them."

"Agreed." Tarron's voice sounded wary, and his posture was alert.

Finally, we reached the top. I turned around to inspect the coliseum below. It was still empty.

Wind blew my hair back from my face, and the place was eerily silent.

"It took you long enough." The voice from my right was oddly high-pitched, with a roll at the end.

I stiffened, turning.

7

About ten feet away, a Satyr stood on two hairy goat legs, his top half naked. A scraggly beard decorated his small chin, and two horns stuck up from his head.

I stepped forward. "I am Mordaca."

He inclined his head. "Fabius."

Tarron joined me. "I am Tarron, King of the Seelie Fae. We seek the Guardians of the Eternal Flame."

"You and that other bitch."

"She's been here?" I demanded.

"Whoa, whoa." He held out his hands, palms facing me. "Don't get pushy."

"I'm sorry." I stepped back, lowering my voice. "She's dangerous and we're trying to stop her from reaching the Guardians. She means them harm."

"Oh, I could determine that." His black eyes glinted. "Sent her the wrong way, I did. And didn't give her the sight."

"The sight?" Tarron asked.

"It would allow you to see what is truly here." He gestured to the stadium, and then to the landscape beyond.

"The people?" I asked.

"And the magic." He nodded. "It's the only way to make it safely to the Guardians. You must be approved and gain the sight."

"How do we do that?" Tarron asked.

"Why, through me, of course."

I waited, hoping he would elaborate.

He didn't.

"What do we need to do?" I ventured in my politest voice. It didn't sound natural on me.

Fabius scoffed, as if he wasn't buying my act. But he continued on anyway. "What are your skills?"

I raised my brows. "A bit of premonition."

I considered telling him I was a Dragon Blood and could do almost any magic I wanted, but decided to hold on to that unless absolutely necessary.

"I am a conjurer and possess the elemental powers," Tarron said.

"Ah, quite nice!" His eyes glittered. He held up a hand and showed us two fingers, like a peace sign. "Two things I would like. From you, Tarron, King of the Seelie Fae, I would like the finest golden lyre in the land."

Tarron nodded. "Done."

"And from me?" I asked.

"I would like you to find me a lady. A satyress. There is

one for me. The gods have told me so. But I haven't found her yet, and I want to know if I must go somewhere to find her."

"You'll play her your lyre?"

"And lure her into my bed!"

Hey, if it worked.

"I can look for that information." And I was willing to lie to him if I had to. I didn't want to, but it would be a small price to pay for saving Tarron and his kingdom. And I could seek him out later to apologize. Maybe even bring Aethelred back to find the lady if I couldn't.

"You first," I said to Tarron.

He nodded and his magic filled the air with the scent of autumn and the sound of wind whistling through the trees. A moment later, he held a perfect golden lyre, which he handed to the satyr.

Fabius took it and inspected it, then strummed a tune.

Instinct made me slap my hands over my ears, and I kicked Tarron. He covered his ears.

The faint sound of the lyre penetrated my hearing, and I swayed.

The bastard was trying to enchant us.

I kicked him hard in the hairy goat thigh, and he stopped, scowling.

Tentatively, I removed my hands from my ears but kept my gaze on his instrument. "I will kick your ass if you try that again."

He harrumphed. "It was worth a try. How did you know?"

"I didn't. Common sense. Don't let some random mythological creature play an ancient instrument. Probably trying to brainwash you."

"Real familiar with brainwashing, are you?"

"You have no idea, pal. Now, are you really going to help us?"

"If you tell me where my lady is."

"I want a blood oath."

"Ugh. Fine." He pulled a little silver dagger from his thigh holster and sliced his arm. I wouldn't make the same vow with him—not the one I'd made with Tarron. For the satyr to spill blood, it would be enough.

I crossed my arms and tapped my foot. "Well, get on with it."

He let the blood drip onto the stones. "I, Fabius the satyr, vow to give you the sight so that you may reach the Guardians of the Eternal Flame. *If* you tell me how to find my satyress."

"Good enough for me." I closed my eyes and called upon my vision.

Surprisingly, this was a lot easier than finding the Guardians. Maybe because less was at stake, since I was prepared to lie if I had to. Almost immediately I saw a satyress sitting by the ocean. It gleamed a perfect blue as cliffs towered around her. A strange rock sat next to her, shaped almost like a lamb. Weird.

I opened my eyes. "I've found her."

"Where? When?"

"I don't know when, but it felt soon. She's at a strange

beach." I described everything I'd seen, hoping he would recognize it.

"Ah, Lamb's Folly Beach."

"Yep, that's the one." I nodded, trying to look knowledgeable. Really, I was just grateful I hadn't had to lie. Been doing too much of that lately.

"Excellent." He rubbed his hands together, eyes gleaming. "I'll be off, then!"

I grabbed his arm. "The sight, remember?"

"Yes, yes." He sighed, then waved his hands in front of each of our eyes. Magic sparked from his palm, and my eyeballs felt warm.

Ew.

I blinked, my vision rapidly clearing.

The coliseum was positively packed. Two gladiators fought in the middle, their armor speckled with red blood and gleaming under the sun. The crowd roared and cheered, blood lust in their tone.

"Ugh." This kind of fight-to-the-death scenario had always grossed me out.

The irony didn't escape me that that's how I'd met Tarron. But at least I'd chosen to fight. Gladiators often didn't.

The crowd nearest us stiffened and turned, as if they finally sensed our presence. Dozens of people dressed in ancient Roman garb stared at us, their brows furrowed.

"Intruders," muttered one.

"Invaders," said another.

"Oh, shit." I looked at Fabius.

He grinned. "I seemed to have forgotten to mention that they can see you, too, now. And they don't like outsiders."

"You bastard."

He shrugged. "But here's some advice you *will* want to follow. There's no reasoning with this lot." He hiked a thumb toward the people who were beginning to stand and approach us. "But if you truly mean the Guardians no harm, then find the Vestal Virgins. They will save your life."

"What?"

"And avoid the storms, whatever you do. And that's all!" He turned and sprinted off.

"The little bastard," Tarron muttered. He drew a sword and shield from the ether. "Let's get the hell out of here."

"Best idea I've heard all day." I called upon my wings, determined to avoid a fight. I needed to save my energy and my power.

I launched myself into the air, the action coming more easily and effortlessly than ever. Wind tore at my hair as I flew high above the stadium. Tarron followed me, his lightning wings sure and strong.

Several of the coliseum patrons had wings of their own, and I was surprised to see pointed ears on a few of them.

"Fae?" I asked Tarron as they approached.

"It seems so. Ancient ones."

"You'd think they'd cut their own kind some slack." I drew an iron blade from the ether for good measure.

A dark-haired Fae wearing a white toga flew for me, his blue wings more like a butterfly's than any modern Fae's wings I'd ever seen. He carried a short sword and round shield. I charged, my blade colliding with his. The sound rang out, and I kneed him in the groin, then pushed off from him. He tumbled off into the distance, and I grinned. That was my new favorite move.

In the distance, Tarron fought two other ancient Fae, his moves swift and sure. Blood arced from their wounds, falling on the coliseum patrons below, splashing them like morbid confetti.

"Leave us the hell alone, or I will kill you." I bared my teeth. "And I'll enjoy it."

The Fae recovered himself, growling and charging. I moved quickly, dodging his blow and slicing my own blade across his neck. Blood spurted and I ducked, keenly aware of my lack of a change of clothing.

His body plummeted to the ground.

Finished with him, I whirled on the air and flew off, searching for other attackers.

Two came from the sides, each headed at me from the opposite direction. One carried a sword, the other a bow. I turned toward the bowman. He drew back an arrow and fired. I raised my shield, letting the arrow crash into the surface. As he reloaded, I stashed my sword and shield back in the ether and drew my own bow. Calling on my dragon speed, I managed to release an arrow right after he did.

My arrow slammed into his, shattering it. I drew another, firing for his neck.

The projectile pierced cleanly, and he whirled through the air, tumbling and turning.

I spun around, nearly face-to-face with the Fae who had been coming from behind. His sword was raised, aimed for my neck.

A dagger appeared from nowhere, slamming into the Fae's skull and sending him flying through the air. He crashed to the ground right between the gladiators. The crowd roared and looked up.

My stomach lurched and my heartbeat thundered. I glanced at Tarron, who had thrown the blade that saved me.

He'd left his own back open while he'd come to my rescue, and the final attacker was raising a huge axe over his head. This time, the figure was a demon, not Fae. His burnished orange body was supported by ebony wings, and his huge horns jutted toward the sky. Yellow goat's eyes gleamed malevolently at Tarron.

My arrow was still nocked. I raised it and released, piercing the demon right through the eyes. He whirled backward.

I hurtled for Tarron. "Let's get the hell out of here."

The entire crowd was now looking at us, and there was no telling how many more of them could fly. I wasn't interested in finding out.

"Bad news." Tarron's tone sounded dire.

I looked down and behind, spotting a hundred winged

beings rising up from the seats of the coliseum. They did *not* look pleased.

"They didn't like that little kerfuffle," I said.

"*Fly.*"

Heart thundering in my ears, I did as he said, stashing my weapon back in the ether and shooting away from the crowd that surged after us. Tarron stayed by my side, his powerful wings moving effortlessly, gleaming like lightning.

"Come on!" Tarron growled.

I flew faster, occasionally sparing a glance at the figures behind. They were gaining.

Damn, they were fast. I needed to practice flying more. Make my wings stronger.

Beside me, Tarron's magic flared. The scent of autumn filled the air. All around, the clouds blackened. They were worse behind us, thunder cracking and rain forming.

I looked at him. "Is that you?"

His brow was twisted in concentration. "It is."

I glanced back. The attackers were slowing, the rain and lightning making it harder to fly. They kept coming after us, seeming determined not to stop, but they were slowing. Elation surged in my chest.

Hell yeah.

We flew as fast as we could, Tarron's magic driving our pursuers back. My lungs burned and my wings ached, but we were gaining. Gaining.

Ahead of us, the sky blackened, even darker than the

clouds behind. It turned to midnight, thick clouds roiling and lightning striking.

"Too much, Tarron!"

"That's not me." Confusion echoed in his voice.

I turned back to look at our pursuers. If some of them were Fae, they might have control over the elements as well.

Every single one of them was turning and fleeing, their faces white.

Holy shit.

I turned back to the storm ahead. It looked even more dire.

Definitely deadly.

Avoid the storms.

That's what the Satyr had said.

And I believed him.

"We need to find shelter!" I shouted.

The storm bore down upon us, traveling miles in seconds. The clouds shifted and swayed, seeming to form the head and shoulders of a man, almost. I blinked through the rain, not sure if I was going blind. The wind howled louder and faster, buffeting me in the air.

"We won't survive this if we're caught out in the open!" Tarron shouted.

I spotted a huge, tumbled pile of rocks down below. A darker section at the base showed where there might be a cave. Lightning stuck, so bright I flinched as it blinded me.

That cave was our best hope.

"There!" I pointed and dived, Tarron right behind.

I flew as fast as I could through the tearing wind, eyes watering and nearly blind. The ground below had turned to mud, and the darkness of the cave beckoned. I flew inside, pulling up abruptly as I nearly ran into the wall.

Whoa.

Shallow cave.

I landed with a stumble and drew my wings back into my body.

Tarron landed gracefully behind me. "Are you all right?"

Gasping to catch my breath, I moved to face him. "Yeah."

He nodded, the concern on his face fading a bit. He turned to the entrance of the little cave and began to conjure a wooden wall to keep out the pelting rain. His shirt was plastered to the broad muscles of his back, making him look even more powerful than usual.

When the wall had been created, he turned back to me, inspecting me from head to foot. "No injuries? You're sure?"

"Nothing bad." Thunder shook the cave around us, and I stumbled. "Holy fates."

Tarron reached for me, pulling me into his arms. The storm howled outside, feeling like it might destroy the wooden wall that Tarron had created.

"This is no normal storm," he muttered against my hair.

I burrowed into his warmth, trying to absorb some of his strength.

Normally, I wasn't into big shows of weakness like this. I liked to stand on my own two feet.

But I also liked being held by Tarron.

I was honest enough to admit it. To myself, at least.

"Storm gods," I said. "Fabius warned us to stay out of the storms."

"We were right to trust his judgment, then."

White lightning illuminated the interior of the cave, slipping through the crack beneath the door.

We stayed like that for minutes or hours, I had no idea. It was probably on the shorter scale, but it felt like ages.

When the cold water began to seep into my boots, I jerked and looked downward. "We're standing in three inches of water."

Tarron shifted as he looked down. "Four inches now."

The water began to rise fast, as if being pushed inside the cave. Maybe that's what was happening—some angry god was trying to flood us out of our little shelter.

Or the whole world was flooding.

The water was nearly to my knees. I looked up at Tarron, panic starting to flutter in my chest. "We need to get out of here."

Face white and lips tight, he nodded and released me. Water was to my thighs by the time he'd blasted the wooden wall away with a great gust of wind. Rain roared in, pelting my face like icy bullets.

He looked back at me. "We're going to have to fight this with the same power its throwing at us."

I nodded, drawing in a deep breath as I followed him

out into the gale. My heart thundered as the cold rain poured. The water was shallower out here—only to my calves. But rising. The world was indeed flooding. Or at least this part of it.

The raging clouds roiled above, black and gray, intermittently lit with blasts of lightning. It struck all around, sending shocks of electric currents that traveled through the water. It wasn't strong enough to knock me out, but eventually one strike might hit close enough.

Fear like I'd never known iced my veins the way the water iced my skin.

As we stepped fully out into the storm, Tarron's magic surged powerfully. The scent of autumn anchored me in the gale.

He created massive blasts of wind, forcing the rain away from us. Forcing the wind away from us. He met the storm god with equivalent power, his hair whipping in the wind and his green eyes turning black with the effort. His wings flared and his horns appeared.

My breath came short. I'd never seen anyone look so powerful before.

I called upon my own magic, slicing my finger and letting the blood flow.

My Fae power wasn't like his—no wind or rain or any other element that I could think of.

But my Dragon Blood magic would allow me to create what I needed. A few droplets of blood dripped into the water at my ankles as I imagined the power of the gale. I used the wind and water around me, drawing strength and inspiration from the storm itself.

It filled me, whirling in my chest and making me feel like I could float off the ground, carried into the sky. When it had filled me to bursting, I let it blast out of me.

More wind shot toward the storm. Then the water. I picked it up, imaging it lifting off the ground and shooting back at the massive clouds that hovered above.

I'd hit the unarmed, faceless storm god with the same thing he'd thrown at us.

Between us, Tarron and I managed to force all the water off the ground, hurling it back into the sky in massive sheets that would crush us if they fell back to earth. We forced the wind away.

Exhaustion tugged at me. Magic flowed from my soul, weakening me with every second. This was truly some spectacular magic, the biggest I'd ever created.

But it was also draining me. Fast.

I'd be on my knees soon.

"Keep going," Tarron roared.

We were almost there.

Exhaustion tugged as I dredged up some strength from deep within, hurling it at the storm as I forced the wind and water away from us.

Finally, the black clouds receded. The wind died down and the rain ceased. An eerie stillness filled the air.

My shoulders sagged. I dropped my arms, letting the magic fade away. Panting, I leaned back on the rock wall behind me.

Tarron lowered his arms, his magic fading from the air. He turned to me, brow creased with worry.

"I'm fine," I said, before he could ask the question. "You?"

He nodded, then raked a broad hand through his hair. His horns disappeared and his eyes turned green once more. Sickly gray clouds swirled in the sky behind him, but they didn't coalesce into blackness once more.

"Come here." He gestured to me. "I'll dry you off."

I arched a brow, wondering how he'd manage it, but not wanting to refuse. Walking in wet leather sucked.

Tarron raised his hands once more, his magic filling the air. A flame appeared from his palms, the heat radiating toward me. It was the perfect temperature, drying my clothes but not burning me. When I was all dry, he turned the magic on himself. Steam rose up from his clothes, and he was fully dry within minutes.

"Thanks." He'd dried me first, and that was definitely the kind of thing I noticed.

He nodded, then turned toward the horizon, searching. "We need to find the Vestal Virgins."

"Agreed. Fabius was right about the storm, so I trust him about this. Even though he's kind of a jerk."

The plateau rose high in the distance, closer than before but still looking dreadfully far.

I called upon my wings. "Shall we fly for a while?"

The mud was still thick underfoot, and I didn't want to tromp through it unless I had to.

Tarron nodded. His own wings burst from his back,

crackling like lightning. We took to the sky, flying over the muddy ground and ragged trees below. The wind whipped at my hair, but it was a gentle breeze, thank fates.

By the time we reached the end of the huge muddy swath created by the flood, I was tiring. Not just my muscles, but my magic. Flying took a fair bit of it, and after the battle with the storm, I was running dreadfully low.

"It's there." Tarron pointed ahead.

I squinted, catching sight of the massive complex of stone ruins. There was something almost threatening about the place. I shivered and flew forward. There was no other option but forward.

8

The white pillars speared the sky, rising up amongst a copse of trees that appeared to have been planted in an ornamental arrangement around the structure.

"Let's walk the rest of the way." I lowered myself to the ground a few hundred yards from the building, grateful to give my wings a rest.

Tarron landed next to me, and we strode through the trees. As we approached the temple, I blinked, clearing the haze from my eyes.

"You see that?" What had once been stone ruins was now a beautiful, intact temple with a dozen white columns and a soaring roof decorated with enormous carvings of goddesses.

"I do."

As we walked up to the front, I was careful to keep my stride relaxed and relatively slow. If someone happened to see us, I wanted to look like a visitor rather than an attacker.

"It's quiet," Tarron said. "But not empty-feeling."

There were no guards, so we continued on, approaching the huge white pillars that were as wide around as ancient redwoods and almost as tall.

Six wide stairs stretched across the whole front, and I strode up them, senses alert. Tarron stuck close by my side. The place had a regal air about it, the architecture fantastic and noble.

It was exactly what I'd imagine for the Vestal Virgins. I didn't know much about them, other than the fact that they were women who'd eschewed love and marriage—and sex—for the opportunity to serve at the Roman goddess Vesta's side, tending her flame for eternity.

Sounded like a bad deal to me. Particularly the no-sex bit. I eyed Tarron beside me. *Especially* that.

Hopefully they wouldn't boot me out. I definitely wouldn't fit among their ranks.

I stepped through the pillars and into a massive stone courtyard. A huge fountain bubbled in the middle, and flowers tumbled down the walls. Their sweet scent filled the air, and I was careful not to breathe in too deeply. No telling what was in the air here, magic or otherwise.

In the corner, about thirty yards away, a woman was making out with a man. Her white robes swept the ground, but the back was cut out to reveal a beautiful tattoo of a bird in flight. They were so into each other that neither of them seemed to notice us.

I glanced at Tarron. "Not what I was expecting."

"No." He shook his head, bemused.

Two figures appeared at the other end of the courtyard, their eyes brightening at the sight of us. They were both tall, beautiful women with an eternally young look—an almost eerie, ethereal beauty—that some immortals possessed. Their white dresses were short and skimpy, an almost modern take on a Roman toga type dress. I wasn't very familiar with proper Roman clothing, but this was *not* it. For one, there was a lot less of it than I'd seen on the statues out front.

One of the women had golden curls piled high on her head, and the other had a long raven mane that was similar to mine when I wore it down. Both smiled widely and hurried forward.

"Visitors!" the blonde one crowed. "How delightful!"

The brunette went straight up to Tarron, her stride quick and her eyes glinting. She wrapped her arms around his neck and plastered herself to his front. "Hello, weary traveler. Won't you come in?"

Oh boy.

The Vestal Virgins were way different than I'd expected.

Annoyance surged in my chest at the sight of the brunette, who looked like she was going to try to climb Tarron like a tree. I wasn't prone to jealousy, but I couldn't help the mean little gremlin that jumped to life inside me. I wanted to snatch her back, but Tarron pulled away from her gracefully. The blonde moved more slowly toward us, and if she went for Tarron—which I was sure she would, from the heated look in her eyes—we were going to have a bit of a problem.

For me, mostly, dealing with this stupid jealousy. Because fighting over a man was *so* not my style, no matter what the gremlin said.

But the blonde woman didn't go for Tarron. She strode right up to me and wrapped her arms around my waist, pressing her body against mine as she gazed into my eyes.

"Hello, beautiful," she purred, blue eyes sparkling.

Okay.

"Points to you for catching me by surprise." Gently, I reached for her hands behind my waist to pry them away.

She laughed gaily. "You thought I would go for your friend?"

"Clearly I was mistaken." And I might not have turned her down once upon a time.

Unfortunately, I was hopelessly hooked on the stupid Fae king to my left, who was trying for a second time to slip out of the grasp of his captor.

"Indeed, you were." She frowned as I pried her off of me. "You're much more my type."

"Thank you. You're not bad yourself. But I'm not quite in the market for that at the moment."

She frowned, drawing her hands back and pouting. She clearly didn't like the concept of personal space, but was willing to respect it. "Then why did you come?"

"Is this the temple of the Vestal Virgins?"

She laughed. "It is, though I'm not sure we're Vesta's virgins anymore."

I glanced at the people making out in the corner. The woman wasn't wearing her top anymore. It draped around her hips, revealing that the bird tattoo covered her arms as well.

"Indeed not." I looked back at the blonde woman. "Change of heart?"

"After a few thousand years of virginity and poking at a little fire for a goddess, yes." The blonde met the eyes of the brunette, who grinned.

"Vesta was all right with this?" Tarron asked.

The brunette laughed. "But of course! She, too, was trapped within the patriarchy of ancient Rome. You don't think this whole virginity thing was *her* idea, do you?"

"If it was…well, internalized misogyny is a bitch," I said.

"Exactly!" The blonde beamed.

"If you're not here to party, why are you here?" The brunette frowned.

"We need information," Tarron said.

"So definitely no partying?" the blonde asked. "I just want to make sure."

I had a feeling that partying was her euphemism for sex. Or whatever was about to happen in the corner of this courtyard.

Yeah, definitely sex.

"We could be up for a party later, maybe," I said. If that

was what these girls wanted, I wasn't above a little sneakery to get the info I needed. And I was *sure* I could find some folks to come back here and party with them if necessary. "But for now, we're seeking something deathly important."

The blonde sulked. "The Guardians of the Eternal Flame."

"The very same."

"Well, come on, then." She waved her hand for me to follow. "Maybe we can work something out."

I shared a glance with Tarron, who nodded.

So far, this wasn't too dangerous. Though that was probably a stupid thing to think. Who knew what these women could pull out?

We followed the Vestal…women…through the courtyard, leaving the couple behind right as they dropped to the ground. Neither the blonde nor the brunette so much as glanced their way.

I hurried up alongside them. "I'm Mordaca."

The blonde smiled. "I'm Aurelia."

The brunette met my gaze, but didn't smile. She wasn't nearly as cheerful as the blonde. "I'm Domitia."

"Nice to meet you."

Both women turned to look at Tarron, Domitia doing it just a little bit faster.

"I'm Tarron." He inclined his head.

"Well, let's take a seat and discuss why you're here." Aurelia led us into a large room with a high ceiling. Huge windows let in shafts of light, and torches burned fragrantly on the walls. A pool of water sparkled in the middle, surrounded by the low Roman benches that were prevalent in the paintings I'd seen.

"We'll call for food," Aurelia said. "You look positively famished."

Alertness tightened my muscles. This was all going *very* easily.

Too easily.

I shared a glance with Tarron, and he seemed to be thinking the same thing.

We followed Aurelia and Domitia to the benches and took a seat. Tarron and I sat on a bench next to each other, while Domitia and Aurelia each reclined on their own. All around, more women and a few men drifted through the space, each of them shooting curious glances at us.

"If you're not the Vestal Virgins, what should we call you?" I asked.

"Vestals is fine," Aurelia said, reaching down to ring a bell.

"And you live here now, throwing house parties?" I asked.

Her eyes brightened. "Exactly! People come from far and wide to join us. And we also protect the location of the Guardians of the Eternal Flame."

It was a handy setup, and I bet they did a damned good job. There were plenty of deadly challenges between the start of this journey and the Guardians. Why not throw in some distraction by pleasure?

A man appeared at our side. He wore a small white

cloth around his waist, and that was pretty much it. A smile of pure delight crossed his face, and he bowed, presenting a tray of food.

"Thank you, Chad. Set it there." Domitia gestured with an imperious hand toward the end of one of the benches.

Chad did as she asked, grinning all the while.

After he left, Domitia leaned toward me. "Chad is new. Traveled quite a way to get here."

"He seems to like his new job."

"Oh, does he ever." Domitia winked. "Some kind of athlete from across the sea. The Americas, I believe. Heathen place. Anyway, Chad showed up, and now he... helps out."

That was one way to put it, I supposed.

And Chad did seem genuinely happy. I hadn't spotted any amulets on him meant to control his mind, and it was usually possible to see when someone was being mind controlled—like the glowing light in the eyes of those that my mother commanded.

Still, there was just something weird here.

Aurelia gestured to the food on the tray. "Help yourself."

My stomach growled, and I realized I was genuinely hungry. Using all that magic earlier had really drained me.

I reached for the tray, but Chad appeared out of nowhere.

He bowed low. "Let me."

Oh boy, this place was weird.

I smiled and nodded. He prepared a plate for Tarron

and me, passing them over. I studied him carefully, and there really appeared to be no magic around him that would compel him to stay.

On the other hand, the Vestals were all beautiful and this place seemed like some sort of sorority house full of women who knew what they liked—sex, mostly—so I could see how this might not be a hardship for Chad.

Subtly, I tried to inspect the food, making sure that none of it was like the Fae fruit that would keep me here forever.

"It's fine," Tarron murmured, so quietly that I could barely hear him.

I trusted him, since he seemed to be an expert on food that could compel you.

Ravenous, I began to eat. The bread, cheese, and fruit was all phenomenal. Though I was aware of the gaze of the Vestals, I ignored it. They chatted away, seeming happy to talk about all the new guys who had shown up on their doorstep in the last week.

A few minutes later, having satisfied the worst of my hunger, I looked up to meet their gazes. They stopped chatting.

"Thank you," Tarron said.

"We need to meet with the Guardians," I blurted. "As soon as possible."

"And why might that be?" Aurelia's keen eyes narrowed on me.

"Another woman"—I didn't want to mention that she

was my mother—"seeks the Eternal Flame. She wants to destroy the entire Seelie kingdom with it."

Both Vestals shuddered.

"*Her.*" Aurelia almost hissed the word.

"You've met her?" Tarron asked.

"Didn't need to," Aurelia said. "Saw her passing by. Bad energy on that one. We hid our home from her so she could not approach."

"That's handy," I said.

"Very." Domitia nodded. "We only want the willing, here."

I glanced at Chad, who waited a few yards away, an eager expression on his face. "Well, success to you, then." Worry over my mother tugged at me. "The woman. How much of a lead does she have on us? I worry what she'll do to the Guardians if they don't share the location of the Eternal Flame."

"Not much of a lead." Domitia grinned evilly. "We sent sprites after her. They will slow her. And she will have a *very* hard time reaching the Guardians without our guidance."

"Impossible, most likely," Aurelia said.

I'd love to think they were right, but I knew it was unlikely. "Don't underestimate her."

Aurelia frowned. "No, you are right. That would be stupid."

"You seek the flame to protect it?" Domitia asked.

"We don't seek the flame at all," Tarron said. "Just the

woman who hunts it. We wish to stop her before she gets it and uses it to destroy my kingdom."

Aurelia and Domitia shared a glance.

"Shall we test the truth of their words?" Domitia asked.

Aurelia nodded. "Most definitely." She turned to us then pointed to the pool. "Submerge yourselves."

"I just got dry," I said. "You should have seen the storm out there."

"Do it anyway," Aurelia said. "We need to know if we can trust you, and the pool of truth will reveal that."

"How?" Tarron asked.

"It will drown you if you are lying."

"Effective pool," I muttered, rising to my feet.

These women clearly weren't going to take no for an answer. I strode to the glittering blue water.

"Naked." Aurelia grinned a catlike smile.

I turned to her and raised a brow. "Seriously? This isn't just for your own amusement?"

"Oh, I'll certainly be amused." Her grin widened. "But also, we don't want you polluting the water with your filthy clothes."

"Filthy bodies are just fine." Domitia's smile was full of innuendo, and I nearly groaned.

"You ladies need to get ahold of yourselves," I said.

"I don't see why." Aurelia shrugged.

I didn't want to argue the point with her—and honestly, maybe she was right. Who was I to tell her how to live in her sex temple in the woods? She'd done her time as a Vestal Virgin, so she'd earned it. And I didn't mind getting naked.

Except for the fact that Tarron was here.

I'd rather die than show that I was uncomfortable, though. So I began to strip, starting with my boots.

Tarron rose and mimicked my motions. I made sure to keep my gaze averted. He was a distraction I didn't need. I could feel Domitia and Aurelia's eyes on me as I stepped into the pool. The water was cool, fizzing against my legs though I saw no bubbles. It gleamed an inviting blue as I waded deeper down the stairs.

"Now just think of your intentions," Aurelia said.

"I'm familiar with the drill."

"You've used a pool of truth before?" Interest piqued her voice.

"Something similar." The protections on the chamber beneath our house operated on the same principle, but a pool of truth would just be too much construction work. Not to mention, an obnoxious slowdown when we were in a hurry.

I caught a glimpse of Tarron next to me as I finally submerged. I jerked my gaze away. The last thing I needed was the distraction of his naked body when I needed to be convincing the Vestals I was legit. I banished the memory of his broad shoulders and filled my head with thoughts of my intentions towards the Guardians and the Eternal Flame.

Cool water caressed me, pulling me deeper into the pool as if it had a mind of its own. I submerged, the water seeming to carry me away. It seeped into my mind, the influence of truth swaying my thoughts.

Time passed at a mysterious pace, but my lungs never felt tight. At one point, my hip pressed against something warm and solid—Tarron. I turned toward him, drifting in the current.

We barely touched, but the magic wrapped around us, pressing us closer. I could feel the depth of our connection, the pull of fate and destiny. Warmth flowed through me, the heat of his skin and my own desire.

I drifted toward him, wanting nothing more than to wrap my arms around him. He seemed to feel the same, because he moved toward me and held me tight to his chest. My mouth found his, lips to lips. His strong muscles pressed against me, hot and firm.

Need like I'd never known surged through me. I wanted him. Now.

No.

A little alarm went off in the back of my head. This was a strange time to be kissing. A strange place.

I pulled back, resisting the magic that pushed us together. Tarron clutched me to him, but I pushed harder. Seeming to get the drift, he released me immediately. Through bleary vision, I saw him shake his head, as if trying to drive away the magic in the pool.

A flash of light exploded in my mind.

A premonition. Truth flared to life within my head.

Knowledge.

Only I could save the Seelie kingdom.

And the Unseelie kingdom.

The two of them, together. Neither apart nor the same. My destiny.

Something about me—about my magic—made me the one to do the job.

I gasped, sucking in water. The trance was broken. I surged to the surface, panting and panicked.

9

Tarron burst out of the water next to me, his eyes wide. His dark hair was slicked back from his face, and water droplets glittered on his broad shoulders, gleaming like diamonds on the broad swath of chiseled muscle. "Did you see that?"

"See what?" My mind raced, memories flaring. Had we seen the same thing?

"You're meant to save the Seelie Kingdom. The Unseelie as well."

I nodded. "I did see that."

I turned to Aurelia and Domitia. Both leaned forward, their eyes wide and on us. They looked like they were watching the climax of their favorite soap opera.

They very well might have been.

"Does that pool also show the truth about the future?" I demanded. "Premonitions?"

Aurelia and Domitia both nodded.

"It can show the truth about the future, if someone has the ability to see," Aurelia said. "What did you see? You saving the world?"

For fate's sake, I was sick of seeing the future. I appreciated getting a head start on problems, but I was seeing nothing but misery and responsibility.

"Not the whole world," I said. "And I don't know how it happens. But I did see myself as the Savior of both Fae kingdoms." I shuddered at the weight of the task.

"What does she save them from?" Tarron demanded of them. "The fire? But what will attack the Unseelie Court?"

Domitia shrugged. "We don't know. We put you in there to make sure you weren't lying to us. The premonition is a bonus because she has the sight."

"You're not lying, by the way." Aurelia grinned. "Or you'd be dead."

"If I re-submerge, will I see more?" I demanded.

Domitia shook her head. "The magic is done."

Damn it. I eyed the ground for my clothes, ready to climb out. They were missing. "Where are my clothes?"

Aurelia's brows popped up. "Oh, those? No idea."

I scowled at her. "Cough them up, Aurelia."

She pouted, then reached beneath her cushion and tossed them at me. I climbed out, and Chad hurried forward, handing me a towel that I wrapped quickly around myself. I turned back to Tarron, who was looking studiously away, still standing in the water.

I wouldn't have minded if he'd stolen a peek, but frankly, it was a bit weird in this random sex temple.

As I dried off, Aurelia gestured for me to sit again. I did as she asked, and Tarron joined me once he was dressed. Domitia never once looked away from him, but he didn't seem uncomfortable. Nothing to be embarrassed about for this guy.

His shoulder pressed warmly against mine, and the desire I'd felt in the pool returned. It was natural—I wanted Tarron, there was no denying it—but this was a weird time to be thinking about sex.

These goddesses were the worst.

I looked at the Vestals. "Did that pool make us kiss? Some kind of magic?"

Aurelia shook her head. "The pool of truth makes you do what you want to do most. To face the truth of your deepest desires."

"That's a multitalented pool," I muttered darkly. But it was hard to fight what she was saying. Being with Tarron *was* becoming one of my deepest desires.

"Did you know that would happen?" Tarron demanded, anger slicing through his tone.

"What, you didn't like the kiss?" Domitia's brows rose.

"I like to choose."

"You did choose." Aurelia gestured to the pool. "It's the pool of truth." She leaned forward. "But you know, if I hadn't taken a vow to observe consent when we'd switched the nature of this temple, I might be tempted to use a bit of magic on you."

"Well, don't," I snapped. "The pool was enough."

It probably would have trapped us here if I hadn't come to my wits.

"You know we're telling the truth," Tarron said. "We're here to help your goddess. Tell us how to get to her. Quickly."

Aurelia looked up at the ceiling. The sky appeared through several crystal-clear windows set into the roof. "Well, you won't see her before morning. That is certain."

I frowned. "Why not?"

"The storms are coming."

A cold shiver of dread raced over my skin.

"Fine, then." I knew I didn't want to mess with those, that was for sure. "When can we go?"

"You can leave soon, if you *must*." Aurelia pouted.

"We must. Did you miss the bit about saving your goddess and his kingdom?" I pointed to Tarron.

"Right, right." She nodded. "I get away from myself sometimes." She leaned forward, eyes narrowing. "What will you do for us if we help you?"

"Shouldn't protecting your goddess Vesta be enough?" Tarron asked.

"I'm not entirely sure she needs protecting," Aurelia said. "She can take care of herself."

"Anyway," Domitia said. "We're good at multitasking. We can get a little something for ourselves while we serve our role as Vestals."

"What do you want?" I asked.

Both women raised their brows.

"Right, you've made it clear." I searched my mind. "I know some shifters who might be keen on paying you a visit. I can mention this place to them. Give them directions."

Both women brightened.

"Excellent," Aurelia said. "Getting the word out is quite hard, you know."

"We tried Instagram, but we got the *wrong* kind of attention, if you know what I mean," Domitia said.

Oh, I knew too well. I could only imagine what happened when two beautiful women posted on the Internet that they were looking for some sexy-time fun.

"Yes," Aurelia said. "Make sure they are good-looking. And kind. Smart, too."

"Just use your best judgment." Domitia waved her hand at Tarron. "You did quite a good job picking for yourself."

"Fate picked for me."

"Well done, fate." Domitia smiled.

We needed to get off this topic. "Right. I'll extend an invitation to the shifters on your behalf." Did this make me a pimp? No. No money was changing hands. I was just setting up a blind date. That had a 100 percent chance of sex at the end. "Tell us how to get to the guardians."

"There is a safe way to ride out the storm and to enter the domain of the guardians," Aurelia said. "You must go toward the plateau, as quickly as you can. Before nightfall."

I looked up through the windows in the ceiling. We only had about an hour, from the look of things.

"Situated in the middle of the wall of the plateau,

about a hundred feet off the ground, are some buildings carved right into the rock. There are seven of them. Only one is safe—the middle one. Enter through the door right at the center, but you must give the dirt at the entrance a bit of your blood. Otherwise, it will not grant you access."

"Spend the night there," Domitia said. "Ride out the storm and don't dare to leave before dawn."

"The storms are deadly at night." Aurelia's eyes were serious. "Once they have passed and dawn has approached the horizon, you may travel deeper into the tunnels inside the plateau. These will lead you to the guardians' domain."

"It's underground?" Tarron asked.

"No." Domitia shook her head. "At the termination of the tunnels, you will find stairs leading upward to the top of the plateau. This will get you to the guardians' territory. The path is dangerous, but you must not try to cross overland, out in the open. That is even worse."

"The field of flames surrounds their domain at the top of the plateau," Aurelia said. "Not the flames you are looking for, but deadly all the same. The other woman will have to travel through those."

Thank fates we'd stopped here for help. These women were weird, but I didn't want to get trapped in a storm or travel through a field of flames. Hopefully it would slow my mother enough.

"Do not forget to pay tribute to the building," Aurelia said. "It is ancient. As ancient as the Hittites who once lived here. Respect it, and it shall protect you in return."

I stood. "Thank you."

She inclined her head, then pinned me with a look. "Don't forget to send some nice people back here."

"Will do." I was sure I would have *no* trouble.

Tarron and I hurried out, striding through the courtyards to the exit. I could feel the burning gazes of the two Vestals behind me. Others spotted us as we left, their heads turning and interest glinting in their eyes.

"Let's get the hell out of here," I murmured.

"Couldn't agree more." Tarron strode quickly through the courtyard, and I hustled to keep up.

"Feel like a prime cut of beef at the market?" I asked.

"A bit, yeah."

"Not into it?"

He glanced down at me. "Only if it's you doing the shopping."

I choked out a laugh. "That's the worst pun."

"But you laughed."

"Fair enough." I stepped out into the forest, hurrying down the steps to the leaf-strewn ground.

Tarron joined me, and I met his gaze. "I can't help but wonder where my mother is."

He looked up at the sky, which was darkening. "About to be caught in a storm."

I glanced up. The light was dimming due to the setting sun, but I also spotted the telltale black clouds on the horizon. I shivered. "Let's fly. We'll have all night to rest, and I want to make it there before the first drop of rain so much as drips out."

Tarron nodded, his wings extending. I called upon my own, and we took to the sky.

The evening was cooler and the shadows longer. I ascended above the trees and spun until I spotted the plateau. We were nearly there. The carved building facades right in the middle of the vertical wall called to me. They looked more like artwork than anything else—as if a sculptor had built a scaffold up to the middle of the vertical face of the plateau and carved in the fronts of glorious, classical buildings. Huge pillars and pointed roofs decorated with carvings that I couldn't make out from a distance. Doorways were like little blackened eyes. Instead of walking into an actual building, you would be walking into a cave carved into the rock of the plateau.

Tarron and I flew quickly, outracing the birds who were seeking shelter for the night. They flew with purpose rather than panic, so I had to believe they had somewhere safe to go.

As we neared the plateau, the air sparked with magic. It came from the flat surface, no doubt due to the goddesses. Up close, I could spot the plateau glowing orange at the top.

Tarron pointed and shouted. "Must be the field of flames."

"Thank fates we're not crossing that."

We reached the towering buildings that had been carved into the rock. All seven of them lined up in a row, with shadowed entrances leading deep into the middle of the plateau.

I aimed for the middle one, just like the goddesses had said. It was smaller than the rest, and I landed right on the edge of the entrance, wings whipping at my back. Magic pulsed from the darkened entrance, a barrier that I would need to beg my way past.

Quickly, I sliced my finger with my thumbnail and let a droplet of blood fall to the stone floor below. "Please permit me entrance and protect me from the storm."

The repelling magic flickered and faded, and I stepped forward as Tarron landed behind me. He repeated the ritual and followed me into the darkened cave.

Slowly, I walked through the entryway, arriving in an enormous rectangular room that had been carved out of the rock. There were no windows, of course, but the air wasn't as stale as I would have expected.

"We need light." Tarron called upon a ball of flame, then sent it toward the left wall. It found a wall sconce and zipped inside, lighting the lamp, which shed a golden glow. Tarron created more fireballs, lighting every torch along every wall.

Soon, the entire space glowed golden. Stone furniture had been carved into the space, with plush cushions adorning each bench. I pointed to them. "Courtesy of the Vestals, I imagine."

"That too." Tarron gestured to a wide blue pool right in the middle of the space. It gleamed with a light from within, enchanting.

I strode toward it, bending down to dip my fingers in. "Not a truth pool."

No way I was getting in one of those again.

Tarron joined me, testing the waters with his hand. "Just a bath."

"Thank fates, because I could use one." I caught the sound of rain from outside, and returned to the entry. The sky had blackened fully, and rain poured from the sky. I stood halfway up an enormous cliff face, a thousand feet in the air. It was an amazing place to take in the view of striking lightning and torrential rain. Magic seemed to keep it from coming inside, because every inch of rock at my feet was perfectly dry.

Tarron joined me, and I shivered at the feel of heat radiating from his shoulder. Memories of the kiss in the pool flashed through me, and tension tightened my muscles.

"You're welcome to bathe first," he said. "I'll look for the tunnel exit that will lead us deeper into the plateau."

I nodded. "Thanks."

While Tarron set off to find our path for tomorrow morning, I returned to the pool. He'd conjured two towels and left them there, along with a change of clothes that looked exactly like mine. I touched them, a smile stretching across my face.

It was the little things.

Quickly, I shed my clothes and climbed in, luxuriating in the perfect temperature of the water. The room itself was a bit warm, and the cool blue liquid felt like heaven against my skin.

I leaned back against the edge of the pool, closing my

eyes. I couldn't help but remember the pool of truth back at the Vestals' temple. It had made Tarron and me act on our deepest desires.

And I'd be lying if I said I didn't feel them now.

I did.

I always did.

Not just desire for his physical form—who wouldn't want that? He was perfect. Unbearably beautiful and shaped like a god.

No. It was him I wanted.

Brave and loyal and strong and good.

I opened my eyes, spotting him walking back along the edge of the chamber. He stayed far from the pool, as if he didn't want to interrupt my privacy.

Did I *really* need privacy?

Maybe it was memories of the pool of truth, or the fact that I was stressed out of my mind over what was to come with the Unseelie queen, or the fact that I'd wanted him from the moment I saw him--but I wanted him more than I wanted privacy right now.

More than I wanted just about anything, in fact.

"Tarron," I called.

"Hmm?" His low voice carried across the quiet, golden-lit room.

"Could you come here, please?"

I could see him hesitate. Just briefly. His foot moved forward, then stopped.

I held my breath.

He stepped forward again, striding toward me powerfully. He stopped at the edge of the pool, looming over me, his eyes glued to my own. The water couldn't possibly conceal my breasts, but he was doing his damned best impression of a gentleman.

"Yes?" His voice rumbled, sounding almost rough.

"Would you join me?"

"Join you?" His eyes darkened, going black almost immediately.

I rose from the water, feeling it sluice down my body. "Yes. Join me."

A low groan, almost inaudible, escaped him. But there was no missing the white fangs that flashed in his mouth, or the horns that appeared at the sides of his head. His fists clenched at his sides, and his throat worked.

He was fighting it.

Probably because it was a bad idea to get too far into this.

But he *really* didn't want to resist.

I didn't bother saying any more. My invitation was clear. I wasn't going to beg for it.

He groaned. Within seconds, he'd unclenched his hands. Quick as a flash, he was undressed.

My eyes widened as I took him in. This was the first time I'd had a chance to really look at his body unclothed. Broad swaths of muscles and long limbs. I couldn't get enough of him.

He climbed into the water, moving with the deadly grace of a panther. I started to drift toward him, but I barely had a chance to move. He was on me in an instant, strong hands wrapping around my waist and pulling me toward him as he bent over me, bringing his face closer to mine.

"You're impossible to resist," he murmured against my throat, his breath warm and his lips soft.

I pressed my body full length against his harder one, plunging my hands into his hair as he licked along the column of my neck.

A shiver raced down my spine, and I tilted my head to the side to give him better access. His fangs dragged along my skin, a perfect pleasure pain that made me see stars. When his lips met mine, I gasped.

He kissed me with a hunger that felt like it could never be satiated. His tongue was a miracle, so talented that my breath came short and my skin heated to burning. Tension tightened within me, desire making me shake.

I ran my hands over his strong shoulders, unable to get enough of him. It was all I could do not to wrap my legs around his waist and take this all the way, hard and fast.

He carried me through the water and pressed me back against the stone wall of the pool. His hands and lips were everywhere, making my mind go blank. It pulled me under, until all I knew was him.

10

I ROSE BEFORE DAWN, TENSION MAKING IT IMPOSSIBLE TO sleep any longer. There was no light coming from the door that led to the outside, and the rain seemed to have lessened.

I turned toward Tarron, who slept on the other side of the huge cushion that had been laid out over a stone platform.

We hadn't gotten enough sleep last night. And we'd barely spoken.

I didn't regret a single moment of it.

Sex with Tarron had been pretty much the best thing ever, and I wouldn't regret it. Even when things got difficult.

I poked him. "Wake up."

He blinked, coming awake immediately. His eyes heated as they met mine.

"Dawn isn't far off," I said regretfully. "We need to go."

His eyes cleared, as if he remembered why we were there and everything that stood between us. I still hadn't told him about our future. Guilt tugged harder than ever at me. I would tell him. As soon as we spoke to the goddesses, I would tell him. The guilt burned so strongly that if I had time now, I would.

I swallowed hard and shoved it away, then climbed from the pallet and began to dress. Tarron did the same, moving quickly.

Once we were ready to go, we headed toward the path that he'd found last night. Neither of us spoke. The field of flame would stop burning soon, and we'd need to reach the goddesses.

"Let me." Tarron stepped in front of me, going first into the darkened tunnel.

Unlike the beautifully carved chamber in which we'd spent the night, the tunnel was roughly gouged out of the rock. It was only a few inches higher than Tarron's head, and wide enough that three people could walk side by side. It made it a bit tight to stick right at Tarron's side, but I was stubborn and didn't like the idea of him going ahead of me and facing the danger alone.

No doubt he'd have scoffed at that, so I kept it to myself.

The tunnel was quiet and dark—eerily so. The air became staler the deeper we got, and Tarron ignited a flame in his palm to provide light. As we walked, I began to feel eyes on me. The prickle of attention was impossible to mistake.

"Do you feel that?" I whispered.

Tarron nodded. "Someone is watching."

I turned around, searching the space behind me. A pair of bright white eyes blinked out of existence, disappearing. Definitely a creature, not a person, from the shape of them.

"From behind," I murmured. "Not sure what it is."

"And ahead." Tarron pointed to the left wall in front of us.

I peered at it, spotting the slightest glow of eyes—as if the creature were squinting so they could still see us but not be spotted as easily.

"I think they are little animals," Tarron said.

"Or sprites of some kind."

I debated drawing a blade or shield, and decided against it. They didn't feel threatening. Not yet at least. No need to change that.

"Burn?" I asked to the air. "Could you come here? Don't act like a badass, okay? Try to look nice."

Tarron shot me a curious look.

I shrugged. "The Thorn Wolf can often sense threats. And animals are better at reading other animals."

A few moments later, Burn appeared. His spiked, thorny fur lay against his back in a non-threatening way, and he made a point to wag his tail.

I patted his head. "Good guy. What do you think of the creatures in here?"

He sniffed, then whined with interest. *Bacon.*

"They're fine," I translated, peering into the dark.

Finally, I spotted a little creature with enormous eyes and soft beige fur. The little animal crept forward on little hands with long fingers. It was about the size of a house cat, and looked a bit like a cross between a monkey and a fat-faced rodent. But cute.

Really cute.

One after the other, the creatures climbed from crevices in the rock, moving toward us.

"That's a lot of them," Tarron murmured.

I swallowed hard, my heart picking up speed. They crowded around us, making a weird purring noise. Soon, there were so many that we could hardly walk.

"This could be a problem." Tarron shifted his legs, disrupting twenty little fluffy balls that piled up.

More were coming out of the walls, a tidal wave of them. Little fangs glinted in their mouths, and unease tightened my muscles. I spotted tiny claws on their toes as well. Little, but sharp.

We were surrounded by a couple hundred now, more and more piling on top of each other in their desire to inspect us.

"There are so many that if they turn against us, we're in trouble," Tarron said.

"Totally screwed." I eyed the fangs on a cute one that hung from the ceiling. In half a second flat, these things could turn nasty. There were enough that they could tear us apart.

Worse, we couldn't move forward anymore. There were so many that we were totally stuck.

Tarron created a small gust of wind, trying to blow them back gently. Their little claws dug into the ground and each other, and they didn't budge an inch.

"They're completely impervious," I said.

He tried a stronger gust, and they held firm. Magic glittered around their feet.

Shit.

"They're used to strong wind," Tarron murmured. "They've got some defense against it."

The creatures moved more quickly, jostling against each other. The energy in the tunnel was increasing as the excitement of the little monsters rose.

My heart began to thunder louder. I shifted nervously.

"They're changing," I whispered.

Burn growled, clearly nervous.

Crap, that was bad.

The Thorn Wolf was buried up to his belly in little furry pincushions of fangs and claws. Huge, glowing eyes stared at us from all around.

Four of them were playing with the shiny zippers on my boots, and another two had climbed onto my shoulders to fiddle with the sparkling comms charm around my neck. It clanged against the charm that Aethelred had given me, giving them two things to play with. They seemed delighted, but in a creepy way. Two had climbed onto Tarron to fiddle with the buttons on his shirt, and one clung to my waist, poking at my belt buckle.

"They like shiny things." I could empathize. I was quite the fan myself.

Except they were totally invading my personal space. And there were so many of them now that I thought we might drown in fluffy bodies.

They started to pull at things that interested them, getting more aggressive. They clicked their fangs and hissed.

"I can work with that." Tarron's magic swelled on the air.

"Hurry," I said, twitching as the creatures piled up to my waist. I could feel the pricks of their claws and fangs as they moved more quickly, excited. The energy in the air felt the same as it did before a big storm. Like something bad was going to happen on the turn of a dime.

"I've got it." Tarron's magic prickled from behind.

I turned to look back, spotting a pile of shiny rocks on the ground.

"Look, guys." I pointed, praying it worked. There were so many hanging on to my legs and sitting on my shoulders that I felt weighed down.

Tarron conjured a few more.

Little ears perked up, and hundreds of pairs of glowing, round eyes swiveled to look at the shiny piles of rocks. They glittered invitingly, sparkling in the light of the flame that Tarron held. Then they charged, leaping off of me so their nails dug in.

I winced and cursed.

They flowed as a mass toward the shiny rocks, moving like a wave.

An image of us, buried beneath their fangs and claws

and fluff, flashed in my mind. "Let's get the hell out of here."

Burn disappeared, and we hurried forward.

We were about twenty yards away when Tarron stopped and turned. I mimicked his movements, watching the piles of fluffy murder mice writhe around each other, playing with their trophies. Tarron raised his hands and let his magic fill the air.

A wall of ice formed between us and the creatures, just clear enough that I could see them turn hundreds of eyes toward us, glowing like creepy Christmas lights. Fangs glinted.

"Good thinking." I shot Tarron a look. "We don't need a repeat."

He nodded. "And this way, it will melt and not disturb their habitat."

It was thoughtful of him. What if there were little murder mice babies on this side of the ice wall? If he'd built a wall of stone, they'd starve to death.

That would be a shame. *Not* that I ever wanted to see them again. But still...a shame.

"Good thinking. Wouldn't want the fluffy murder mice to be separated from their babies," I said.

Tarron shot me a look, brow raised. "Fluffy murder mice?"

"You know, big eyes, little fangs."

"Oh, I followed. I just think they should be called killer kittens." He grinned, then nodded his head toward the tunnel. "Let's get out of here."

We turned and hurried forward through the tunnel.

"We must be getting close," Tarron said. "It's been miles."

"Fates, I hope you're right."

When the earth began to shake around us, I hoped even harder. "What's that?"

"Feels like an earthquake." He reached out, steadying himself against a wall.

"This region isn't known for them."

"Magic, then."

"My mother?" Terror sparked in my chest. She could be above ground right now, wreaking havoc.

Dust fell from the ceiling as the earth shook harder.

"Run!" I sprinted forward, skin cold with fear.

Tarron raced alongside me. I sliced my finger as his magic flared. The trembling minimized a bit, and I added my magic to his, imagining myself controlling the rock walls around us. Keeping them firm and in their place.

Please don't fall and crush us.

I pushed my magic as hard as I could, trying to keep the walls from shaking. Tarron's power surged, filling the tunnel with the scent of an autumn day and the sound of wind whistling through the trees. My lungs burned as we ran, trying desperately to reach the stairs I prayed were ahead of us.

Dirt and rock chips continued to rain down, and my legs felt like jello as the earth shook.

"Nearly there," Tarron said.

"You can tell?"

"Can smell fresh air."

I put on a burst of speed as the ground shook harder. This was my mother. I knew it.

Finally, I spotted the stairs ahead of us. They were roughly carved out of the rock and extremely steep. I sprinted up them, Tarron right behind me. At the top, a huge slab of rock blocked my way. A tiny sliver of space allowed fresh air and light through, but the white rock itself was enormous.

I pressed my shoulder against it, heaving with all my strength. The Dragon Blood that flowed through my veins gave me extra strength. The rock budged. Tarron joined me, shoving his huge body against the stone and pushing. My muscles burned as I kept up the pressure, hoping our combined strength could do it.

As the earth shook around us, we managed to shove the rock away enough that we could scramble out. Tarron pushed me out first, heaving me up with two strong hands against my butt. I scrambled out into the sunlight and into chaos.

We were at the edge of the temple, in an area surrounded by the charred soil of the field of fire. Only a few yards from us, the ruins of the temple gleamed white in the sun. One of the columns had fallen into the field of fire, blocking the tunnel exit.

A battle raged ahead, magic and blades flying through the ruins of an ancient Greek or Roman temple. I hurled myself behind the cover provided by an enormous, fallen marble column and curled up. Tarron joined me a half second later. We were surrounded by huge pieces of fallen marble.

I blinked, trying to clear my vision and use the gift that the satyr had given me. The ruins did not turn themselves into a fully formed temple.

"I think she's destroyed the place," I said.

"He has." Tarron pointed to the same enormous Fae that had hit me with a blast of debilitating energy magic yesterday.

He threw blasts of energy at the remaining parts of the goddesses' temple. Enormous pillars crashed to the ground, shaking the earth.

"He could collapse the tunnel on the fluffy murder mice," I said.

He moved into a crouch, ready to leap up. "I'll take care of him. We should stick together."

"Sure." I so wasn't going to do that. I knew he wanted to protect me, but I had to find my mother before she got the information she'd come for.

Tarron charged forward, wings spreading majestically from his back as he conjured a sword and shield. Now that he had the giant in his sights and wouldn't be caught unawares like last time, I knew he'd be fine.

I conjured my own shield and followed him. When he'd passed through a stone arch, I deviated and went left, slipping between two pillars that still stood upright. The sound of screams drew me forward through the rubble. My mother's scent—putrid night lilies and brimstone—made me gag. The fallen pillars and giant blocks of marble made the temple into an obstacle course, and I climbed over and ducked under huge white stones.

A flash of movement to my right caught my eye, and I whirled. From behind a pillar, a tall Fae lunged at me. His dark hair and pale skin gleamed under the dawn sun, and he raised a slender obsidian blade.

His eyes glinted with malice as he threw it, and the black glass sparkled in the sunlight. I raised my shield and ducked behind. The glass shattered against the metal, and I dropped my sword, drawing my own dagger from the ether. I went for steel, willing to pull no punches when I was so close to my mother.

I peeked out from behind my shield and threw my blade. The Fae darted right, so fast he managed to nearly avoid my dagger entirely. It stabbed him in the shoulder, and he howled, clutching at it.

Quickly, I grabbed my sword and charged, leaping over a pile of rubble and taking to the air with my wings. I flew fast and low. The Fae's eyes widened, and he called on his own wings, rising up into the air as he grabbed another dagger from a holster at his thigh.

I was faster than I had been, the practice clearly having paid off. We collided five feet above the ground. He swiped out with his dagger, but I darted right. The blade sliced shallowly at my arm, burning like hell but not debilitating. I stabbed him through the middle with my sword, and he shrieked.

Roughly, I jerked the blade free and kicked him away.

He fell and slammed to the stones below. I turned and flew back to the ground, spotting Tarron in the distance.

He was fighting the huge Fae who sent the deadly blasts. Tarron's sheer power and speed were incredible, and he landed a kick to the Fae's face that sent him spinning. More Fae surged toward him, raising weapons.

As much as I wanted to keep watching or fly over to help, I didn't want to stay too high in the air where I could be seen. The cover provided by the ruined temple was too good to pass up, and I still needed to find my mother.

Tarron could take care of himself. And while he distracted most of the Fae with his huge, loud fight, I'd take out the queen.

Quietly, I crept through the ruins, keeping low as I moved closer to my mother's dark magic. It took everything I had not to race forward—but if I did, I'd have to lower my shield. I couldn't afford to get hit by one of her mind-controlling potion bombs. Not when I was so close to her.

I found two more Unseelie along the way, managing to narrowly avoid death both times. As I got closer to my mother, the skill of her guards increased.

Smart.

But then, it probably ran in the family.

I reached a clearing in the middle of the temple. Here, the pillars were far enough away that my mother had found some space to work. Her magic was so strong that she had to be within only a few yards of me. I crouched behind a huge block of marble and peered out.

The sight before me dropped my stomach to my knees.

I could see the backs of the four goddesses, each of whom knelt on the ground in front of my mother. All four goddesses were surrounded by an individual bolt of white, electric energy. It extended from a two-foot tall crystal shard that had been plunged into the ground in front of them, somehow holding them tethered. My mother stood in front of the crystal, grinning malevolently.

"I'll know what you know soon enough," she murmured.

The goddesses fought, jerking against their lightning chains, but they could barely move.

I could hear Fae attackers all around, ransacking the temple or fighting Tarron. But there were none around my mother. She was confident in her ability here.

She probably didn't even sense me yet, so enraptured was she with her victory over the goddesses. But she hadn't gotten the information yet.

I had time.

I drew my bow and arrow from the ether and raised it, getting my mother in my sights. I pulled back on the string, then released.

The arrow flew true and straight.

I held my breath.

It slammed into my mother's chest, then disintegrated. There wasn't even a burn mark on her pale skin.

Her eyes flashed up, wide and enraged. "Who's there?"

I hid, silent. I needed another damned plan.

"Daughter?" She sniffed the air, then tilted her head. "Ah, yes. I believe that must be you."

Shit. Powerful, miserable hag.

I frowned, mind racing. The only power I had against her was reflecting her magic. She'd probably be prepared for that.

A blast of energy smashed into the marble block behind which I hid.

I flinched back as it slid toward me, shards of stone flying off the front.

"I'll drive you out!" she shrieked.

Another blast of energy hit the stone, nearly destroying it.

Shit. One more blast and I'd lose my cover.

And she was stealing the information from the goddesses as we spoke. Every delay was dangerous.

My eyes darted to the streams of energy that trapped the four kneeling figures.

If I could reflect a magical attack back at the attacker, maybe I could even divert magic.

I charged forward, hiding behind my shield.

With everything in my soul, I prayed to fate that this worked.

My mother shrieked and sent a bolt of power right at me. It slammed into my shield, nearly making my arm go numb. Clumsily, I tightened my grip so I didn't lose it. I could try to reflect her magic back at her, but I didn't want to drop my shield in case she had one of those potion bombs.

When I neared the electric current, I lunged for it, reaching out my hand and bracing myself.

My fingertips collided with the bright white light, and energy zipped through my veins. With all my strength, I threw my shield at my mother, and it smashed into her, making her shriek. The energy coursing through me almost froze me solid, but I forced it out of me, channeling it through my other arm and out my fingertips.

Please work.

I directed the stream of white light at my mother, who was rising from beneath the metal shield that had knocked her to the ground.

The light crashed into her chest, and she shrieked. Something small hit me in the back, startling me but not slowing me down. I forced the magic toward my mother, who went to her knees.

She gave me a vicious look, then one of triumph.

Fear tore at my heart.

Then she disappeared.

Shit!

I dropped to my knees, yanking my hand from the stream of current as pain surged through me. Weakness followed. Horrible dizziness.

But the goddesses were still trapped. I crawled for the crystal that was still stuck in the ground. It continued to shoot the electric light at the kneeling figures. With my remaining strength, I drew a massive ax from the ether. I rarely used this one, but kept if for special occasions.

Rising to my knees, I slammed the ax into the crystal.

The shock reverberated up my arms, but nothing happened.

I was too weak.

Darkness began to close in around me.

Through bleary vision, I saw Tarron appear. He hurtled from the sky like an angel of death, fear and anger on his face. Blood speckled all of his visible skin, and his clothes looked soaked with it. He landed and conjured a huge mallet, then swung it at the crystal.

The thing shattered into a million pieces. The white light faded.

I collapsed. As darkness took me, the edges of my mind processed what had hit me in the back.

Potion bomb.

11

I struggled toward consciousness, my mind fuzzy. The ground was hard beneath my back, the warm air scented with blood.

I was swept up into a pair of arms.

Strong arms.

It had to be Tarron.

He was warm and solid against me, clutching the top half of my body to his.

Groggily, I opened my eyes. Before I could even focus on his face, agony stabbed me in the stomach. I gasped, going blind.

The first thought—the crazy thought—was that Tarron had stabbed me.

But no.

Not possible.

Not after last night.

Then the gnawing need came—*I had to go to my mother.*

It raged through me, a ferocious desire to tear myself out of Tarron's arms and run to her. To transport to her. To do whatever it took to get to her side and serve at her command.

Faintly, noises penetrated my mind. Footsteps, a rustling sound, Tarron's voice. "She's been hit with a potion."

I was jostled, the pain shooting from my stomach as my clothes were torn off me. Cold water doused me, front and back. I sputtered, trying to blink my eyes open. To tear myself away from the overwhelming dark desire that blacked out everything else.

Through bleary eyes, I spotted Tarron looming above me, his wet hands hovering over my chest. Concern creased his brow and glinted in his eyes. Water poured from his hands as he washed me clean.

"We have to get the potion off," he said, his voice sounding desperate.

"I'm afraid that won't work," a feminine voice said from behind me. It resonated with power that vibrated my bones.

One of the goddesses.

I shuddered.

"Here, let me." Another feminine voice.

A figure appeared at the corner of my eye. She was beautiful and pale, with golden hair and a simple white dress decorated with glinting thread that matched her hair.

I fought to get away from her, somehow sensing that she would try to drive my mother's influence from me.

"No!" I gasped and clawed, even as my subconscious fought within me, some deep little part of my mind screaming for me to shut up and let her help.

"Be still." Command echoed in Tarron's voice as he gripped my arms and held me down.

The goddess touched my arm, her fingertips burning hot. It streaked through me like fire, lighting up my veins. I screamed.

Agony.

Pure agony.

But my mind cleared.

It was as if she were burning my mother's influence out of me.

"That should help," she murmured.

I lay limp, gasping. Sweat chilled on my skin, and my mind returned to itself.

My situation came to me in a rush, and if I could have dropped my head back to the ground in despair, I would have. Except I was already lying down. Naked. Soaking wet.

Shit.

This was the worst.

If my clothes and makeup were my armor—which they were—they'd just been chucked into the trash.

I stiffened my spine and pressed my lips together.

Damn it, there was no time for weakness. I drew in a steady breath and opened my eyes, finally able to see clearly. I could still feel the tug of my mother's magic—stronger than ever—but I was able to control it.

"Hello." I smiled at the goddess, deciding to ignore the fact that I was weak as a slug and lying naked on my back, soaking wet. "You must be one of the guardians."

She gave me a bemused look. "Indeed I am."

"Well, I'm sorry I was late." I rose, slowly sitting upright as every bone in my body ached. I gestured to Tarron, my hand palm up and open.

He seemed to get the gist and conjured me a robe. It was black silk, with a plunging neckline and severe lapels.

Well, at least he got me.

I stood and swung the robe around my shoulders, straightening them as I turned to face the four goddesses.

They looked *pissed*.

And ragged. Each had frizzy hair from the lightning and pale skin, their pupils wide and dark. Burn marks singed their clothes, and they smelled faintly of smoke.

Tarron stood, concern radiating from him like an aura. "Are you all right?"

"No, I suspect I'm not." I shuddered, the sensation of my mother's magic inside me making my insides feel like they were coated in slick black oil. I moved my gaze from one goddess to the next. "But I suppose you can tell us exactly how *not all right* we are?"

"We were trying to stop that woman from learning the location of the Eternal Fire," Tarron clarified.

"Oh, we know," the blonde goddess said. Her sweeping white dress and the laurel wreath around her head looked vaguely Greek. She must be Hestia.

"You almost stopped her," said the redhead. "Almost." She wore a brilliant green dress to match her eyes, and her hair looked like it'd be pretty curly even without the electric energy. A Celtic tattoo twined itself around her collarbones—beautiful, delicate knots that had to symbolize something important. She must be Brigid.

"She got the information she came for."

Shit.

The woman who had spoken was a brunette with beautiful golden skin and midnight eyes. Her clothing was unfamiliar—blue silk that wrapped around her in sweeps of shimmering fabric. She had to be Arinitti, the Hittite goddess.

The last woman—one with pale brown hair and a distinctly Roman toga and nose—crossed her arms and frowned, a seriously peeved look on her face. Vesta, the Roman goddess.

Dread opened a hole in my chest as the reality of our situation struck me.

We'd failed. And the goddesses were pissed.

"Who are you?" demanded Vesta.

I stepped forward. "I am Mordaca, a Blood Sorceress and the daughter of the woman who just stole information from you."

It was probably a bold move to admit it, but I didn't want to hide it.

"Took it right out of our heads," Brigid spat. "That crystal of hers was impossible to fight."

"What does she want it for?" asked Hestia, the blonde goddess. Her gaze moved between me and Tarron. "It must be for something she plans to do to the two of you, if you're so keen on stopping her."

I nodded sharply. "She plans to destroy his realm with it."

Brigid nearly growled. "If she releases that flame, it will kill hundreds. Thousands. It travels like the wind, destruction incarnate."

"I told you we should have protected it better," snapped Arinitti.

Vesta gestured around. "Look, Arinitti. Just look. How much better could we have done?"

I followed her gesture, inspecting the area around us. Dozens of stone statues of warriors lay broken around us. Maybe a hundred. They must have been the forces fighting the Unseelie. That's why I hadn't seen them. They'd blended in so well with all the white stone around them, and I'd been so busy trying to stay alive that I hadn't noticed them at first—I'd had eyes only for the Unseelie attackers or my mother. Even now, she pulled at me.

Shaking, I reached for Tarron's hand and gripped it tightly. More than anything, I needed to remain mentally present *here*. In this reality. Not in some crazy half world of compulsive magic that my mother had cast me into with her potion bomb. I'd like to go back and kill whatever Unseelie had hit me with it from behind.

It took everything I had to fight her pull on me. Considering that I had the power to transport to the entrance of the Unseelie Realm in a heartbeat, I almost didn't trust myself.

"It's nearly inconceivable that she made it here," Vesta said. "She was insanely powerful. We had a guard of a hundred stone warriors—not to mention our own powers—and she still triumphed. It's impossible to plan for that."

I sort of disagreed, but I kept my mouth shut. We needed info right now, and we needed to be quick.

"Can we stop her?" I asked. "Track her to the Eternal Flame?"

"You can." Hestia stepped forward, her footsteps faltering. "You must. We are too weak."

Brigid scowled, as if she didn't like that assessment, then she lifted her hand to her head, clearly in pain. "I hate to agree with her, but she is right. Whatever was in that harpy's magic has weakened us. We will go after her as soon as we are able, but I'm afraid that may take time."

"We don't have time," Tarron said.

"Indeed, you do not." Arinitti frowned at us. "You made it safely through the trials protecting this place."

"We did. Which is why you should tell us—immediately—how to get to the Eternal Flame so that we can stop my mother."

Arinitti's dark brows drew together over her forehead. "You will not use it for yourself?"

She was clearly the suspicious one in the group.

Couldn't blame her, after what my mother had done to her home.

"Only if it allows me to kill her." I shrugged. "And yeah, running around with Eternal Fire and lighting stuff up isn't really my style."

"We went into the Vestals' pool of truth to prove we aren't after the flame itself," Tarron said, apparently deciding to go with more tact than I'd used.

Vesta nodded. "I can feel that."

"Good, then—" I doubled over. Pain shot through my stomach again, and that familiar gnawing ache ignited inside me. I gasped, tryin to get ahold of myself.

The queen had called.

I have to go to her.

I straightened, the urge consuming me.

"She's at it again." Arinitti grimaced.

Bitch.

All the same, the ether tugged at me. As if my transport power wanted me to make the pain stop by going to her.

"Let me." Hestia stepped forward, reaching out to press her fingertips to my shoulder. Her touch drove away some of the pain and the horrible compulsion.

I straightened, breathing more slowly. "Is there any way for you to stop it entirely?"

She shook her head, her eyes dark. "There is a potion, but I do not have the ingredients. It would give you enough control to resist her call, but I don't know that it would cure you."

A potion.

Connor was looking for the antidote. Perhaps he'd found the one she spoke of.

I nodded. "Thanks. What can you tell us about getting to the Eternal Fire? We need to hurry."

"The fire is located at Mount Chimaera," Arinitti said. "It has been there for over a thousand years, undisturbed."

"Mount Chimaera?" Tarron frowned. "Like the beast with a lion's head and a snake's tail?"

"Don't forget the goat head growing out of the middle of its back," I said. "That thing is *real*?" It had always sounded too crazy to me, an ancient myth created in a time without TV.

"Not the creature, no," Arinitti said. "The creature took its name from the mountain, which is populated by lions, goats, and snakes."

"And some ancient philosopher historians just smooshed them all together to make a weird animal?" I asked.

Vesta scoffed. "Indeed. Morons."

"In fairness, one of them got it right." Hestia tapped her chin, then shook her head. "I can't recall his name, but it doesn't matter. You must make your way past these creatures to get to the top. They will try to stop you."

"Do you have any advice for that?" Tarron asked.

After our encounter with the fluffy murder mice, I couldn't blame him for asking. Even the cutest creatures could be deadly if there were enough of them. I didn't even want to discover how a bunch of goats could turn on us.

Vesta stepped forward. "You must go to the village of

Amata. There, you will find a shepherd by the name of Devrim. Pay him, and he will help you reach the base of the mountain where you will find the safest route to the top."

"Do *not* deviate from that route," Arinitti said.

"What do we pay him with?" Tarron asked. "Is there anything particular he wants?"

"This." Arinitti stepped forward, then yanked out a piece of her hair. She handed the perfect black strand to Tarron, who took it with a frown. "A goddess's hair is valuable currency in some circles."

Tarron nodded, then conjured a small metal box and placed the hair within. He slipped it into his pocket.

"The lions," Brigid said. "You must not kill them. They are the last Asiatic lions in Turkey. The rest were hunted into extinction in the nineteenth century."

I wasn't keen on killing any furry critters—but especially endangered ones. Still, I frowned at her. "Is there anything we can do to get them to let us pass without harming us?"

She shrugged. "Be creative."

Okay. That wasn't the best advice, but I was glad she'd at least told us about them. So far we'd gotten help from three of the four goddesses.

I looked to Hestia, who stepped forward. "One more gift."

She hovered her hand over my shoulder once more, and I nodded.

Lightly, she rested her fingertips on my skin. Warm

magic flowed into me, racing up my neck and into my mind.

I shook my head, getting used to the strange feeling. "What was that?"

"You will see." She smiled and stepped back.

I forced myself to smile gratefully, even though I wanted to make an annoyed quip about the pointlessly enigmatic nature of goddesses.

"You must be careful," Hestia said. "The magic that is drawing you to the Unseelie queen is extremely powerful. You may need to be chained to keep from going to her."

I grimaced. "Could I just block my transport magic?"

I had no idea if that was even possible.

"Perhaps," Hestia said. "If you have a charm to do so."

There was probably no time to find one. *Please have an antidote, Connor.*

"Do you know how to break this magical chain on her?" Tarron asked.

"A bit of the queen's blood could do it," Hestia said. "Put it into an antidote."

Add that to the to-do list of misery. "Or I could just kill her."

"That would be the most effective method, yes." Hestia nodded.

"Great. Thanks." Fabulous advice.

"You must go," Brigid said. "The queen will receive no aid in reaching the top of the mountain as you have, but she may achieve it all the same."

"Not if I have anything to say about it." Arinitti glowered.

"You'll send something after her?" I asked. Arinitti was the perfect one to do it. As a Hittite goddess, Mount Chimaera was in her territory.

"Oh, yes." Her eyes glowed with an unholy light. "The wrath of our ghosts and myths."

I sure wouldn't want to be on the wrong side of that.

"Go," Brigid said. "The queen's power was unlike anything I've ever seen. She may not be slowed much. It is up to you to stop her."

I nodded, swallowing hard.

Talk about pressure.

"We will create a portal for you," Vesta said. "You should not use your transport magic until you are out from under her spell. If it overtakes you while you are in the ether, you might try to transport yourself directly to her."

That would be literally the worst.

I nodded. "Thank you."

The goddesses combined their magic to create a shimmery silver portal.

"Where to?" Hestia asked.

"Potions & Pastilles, on Factory Row in Magic's Bend."

She nodded, then flicked her hand toward the portal. It glowed with golden light. "You may enter. And good luck."

"Thanks." We were going to need it.

Tarron reached for my hand and gripped it tight, and we stepped into the portal at the same time.

Just as we stepped in, I heard Brigid's voice. "Be careful.

All is not what it seems."

Then the ether sucked us in. He kept a tight hold on me as the ether spun us through space. What the hell did she mean by that?

We arrived in front of Potions & Pastilles. The street was dark and quiet, chill with the early morning air. The shop itself was empty save for the glowing lights within, which gave it a feeling of life even though no one was inside. Quickly, I waved a hand in front of my face, using a bit of magic to clean myself up so it appeared I was dressed the way I normally did.

There was power in appearances, and I wouldn't give up mine. Connor was a friend, but still. I liked to be put together—or to look that way, at least.

I knocked on the glass door, praying that Connor was still up. For a moment, there was no response. I knocked harder.

"Coming!" The voice sounded from above, and I looked up to see Connor leaning out of a second-story window. "Mordaca!"

"Hey. Any chance you have that antidote?"

He grinned, but it didn't go all the way to his eyes. "Half an antidote."

"Better than nothing."

The grin spread a bit wider. "I'll be right down."

Tarron and I stood on the doorstep, waiting. Silence thickened the air. It was the first time since I'd woken that we weren't running for our lives. And a hell of a lot had happened.

The night before played through my mind. Today, too, and the knowledge that we'd missed my mother by a hair's breadth.

She might get the flame.

I swallowed hard.

To distract myself, I pressed my fingertips to my comms charm. "Aeri? We're at P & P. Any chance you can meet?"

"Finally. Been waiting to see you. I'll be there in fifteen minutes."

"Thanks." I cut the connection.

Connor swung the door open and gestured us inside. "Just give me a few minutes, okay? I need to take it off the burner, but I think it's ready."

"What will it do?" I asked. "I've been hit with another dose, so I need something strong."

He blanched. "Another?"

"Just now."

"Shit. Well, this will help. It won't get her influence entirely out of your system—you'd need a bit of her blood for that—but it will help you resist her call."

"It'll have to do. Thanks."

He nodded and hurried off, calling over his shoulder as he disappeared into the room behind the counter, "Help yourself to anything."

Instead of finding food or drink, Tarron and I just stood there. It was like the shock of the last twenty-four hours was catching up with us. Me, especially, now that I was back on familiar ground.

Apparently I'd lost my mind when I'd slept with him. "So. The elephant in the room."

"Last night?" he asked.

"That's it."

"What of it?"

Weirdness slipped over my skin. I felt like I was trapped—between my feelings for him and the looming threat provided by my mother. By the lies that I could no longer keep. Yet I didn't know how to say. Frustration made me feel like I was going to burst.

So I said something that wasn't entirely true. "I just hate this fated mates thing. It's so hard to trust that we're in control of our own actions. That you really want me and it's not just fate driving you."

He laughed, a slightly weary sound. "Hardly."

I scowled at him.

His gaze, when it met mine, was hot with banked fire. "I would want you if we were fated enemies."

"We kind of are, aren't we?" The memory of the premonition flashed in my mind. "How could we possibly be fated mates, considering who my mother is and what she is trying to do?"

He strode toward me and gripped my shoulders, pulling me close. The tortured frustration that radiated off of him was so strong it was nearly visible as an aura. "You drive me insane, Mari. Your mother is literally my greatest enemy, responsible for the death of my only family. But you? No. You are not my enemy. *You* are my *Mograh*."

I drew in a shuddery breath.

"Discipline is my life," he said. "In every aspect, I have no problem doing what I must."

That was an understatement. He didn't want to be king. Never had. Yet he let his entire kingdom think he had murdered his brother for the throne, solely so he could preserve his brother's legacy and protect his kingdom. He had crafted it specifically so they *would* believe that.

"And yet with you, I can't fight what's happening between us." His voice sounded torn from his throat. "And I don't know that I want to try."

I didn't want to either. Part of me wanted him forever, which sounded crazy. But I couldn't have it. Not as long as I was fated to kill him.

Guilt flashed through me.

Fates, I'm a mess.

A total, freaking mess.

I met his gaze, my heart thundering. "It's fate making you say these things."

I hated this fated mate connection. It made it even harder to trust the one you were falling for. Were his feelings real, or manipulated by some cosmic connection? Was it just fate meddling or his own emotions?

My own emotions? I didn't want that bitch making decisions for me.

"It's not." Intensity shined in his gaze. "It's you. Fated connection or no, it's you."

I scowled at him. "How can I trust that?"

"You're smart and strong and stubborn and a bitch. And I like it."

"That's supposed to be a compliment?" I asked the question, but the truth was, it sure sounded like one to me. Bitches got shit done.

"The highest compliment. I don't want a weak woman. Or a nice woman. I want a fighter. One who does the right thing, even when it's hard."

"I'm not nice?"

He shook his head. "No. You're kind. There's a difference. One is a social tool; the other is real. You are real. And I want you, no matter what fate says."

Warmth ignited inside me.

I wanted him, too. *Liked* him, too. Like his reluctant leadership of the Seelie kingdom. The sacrifice he'd made for his brother. The way he was kind to Burn.

The realization made my heart flutter. Panic followed close on its heels.

The world was bearing down on us, and every vision I'd had of the future was *bad.*

I couldn't fall for him right now. Couldn't be distracted from what lay ahead of us.

"I'm fated to kill you!" I burst out, determined to drive him off this path. Determined to finally tell the truth, now that I was running out of time to change the future. I pulled back, my mind racing. "I thought I could stop it. But I don't know if I can."

"What?" Confusion flickered in his gaze.

"Tarron. I'm fated to kill you."

12

He frowned, disbelieving. "Explain."

His tone was neither angry nor frightened—though to be honest, I wouldn't have expected fear from him.

I recounted the vision I'd been keeping to myself, feeling guilt washing over me. This was a *huge* lie.

"But it may not even happen," he said. "Aethelred said that we don't know if you see the one true future or a possible future."

"Right. But it *could* happen."

"But it hasn't."

"I lied."

"You omitted." His brow furrowed. "I can't abide the lies, but this isn't the same as hiding the past or something you know for certain."

"It feels the same."

He gripped my hand. "I—"

Connor entered the room through the door behind the counter, and I jerked.

I'd totally forgotten where we were.

Holy fates, we'd just had this conversation in an empty P & P.

"I've got it here..." Connor's gaze moved between our faces. He frowned briefly, then clearly decided he would just forge on. "You'll be feeling better in no time. Not perfect—not until we get some of her blood to fully break the curse—but definitely better. More yourself."

"Less like an evil minion?"

"Precisely." He smiled, his dark hair flopping over his forehead as he looked down at the vial in his hand. "I'm afraid this doesn't taste very good, however."

"They rarely do."

I approached and took the little blue vial from him. "Thank you so much. You really are a lifesaver."

He shrugged. "It's not that different from making cocktails really."

"Those are also a lifesaver." And damned if I wouldn't love a Manhattan right now.

That was a long way off, however.

I swigged back the potion, feeling Tarron's eyes on me. I shuddered as the sour taste exploded on my tongue, then handed the vial back to Connor. "Thanks."

He nodded. "Anytime. Can I get you anything else?"

My stomach grumbled. Now that I'd partially come down from the terrifying high of seeing my mother and confessing to Tarron, I could feel the ravenous ache.

"Food." Connor grinned. "No problem."

He returned to the space behind the counter and began to fiddle around with things. I turned back to Tarron, surprised to see him still watching me and seemingly unconcerned.

He really wasn't that bothered about the killing thing—no doubt because he thought it wouldn't happen—and he was only partially ruffled by the lie.

I shook my head slowly, perplexed.

His gaze swept down my body. "You need some real clothes."

"It's a bit hard to fight battles in a bathrobe, yeah. Not that I'm not up to it, of course."

"Course not." He conjured me a set of my usual clothes and boots.

"Thanks." I took them and headed to the bathroom, then changed quickly and ditched the robe in the cabinet below the sink. It was too nice to throw out. Maybe I'd come back to get it.

Dressed, I returned to the main part of the bar. Aeri rushed into the room a moment later, the front door allowing a gust of wind to enter the bar.

"Well?" she demanded, her gaze bright.

"We have our work cut out for us." I frowned.

"I'm going to check in with the Court Guard while you two catch up," he said.

I watched him walk toward the corner of the room, then turned my attention to Aeri. "Tell me you found a way to keep me from having to kill Tarron."

"I don't know that I have, but I've at least found out *why* you might have to kill him." Worry entered her eyes. "Does this mean that your mother got the location of the Eternal Flame."

"She did." Anger twisted my insides, and regret. Regret for the fact that I had been born to such a sociopath, even though I couldn't have controlled that anyway. "We need to go to Mount Chimaera to stop her, as soon as possible."

"Okay, well, first, you need to talk to this Fae historian that I met while helping Luna find reinforcements to protect the Seelie Court."

"We don't have time."

"He's right there." She turned and pointed to a slender man who waited outside, shifting impatiently from foot to foot. "He's the reason I couldn't come right here. I needed to go get him. I've left Declan with Luna to keep helping."

Declan was her boyfriend, and he'd probably do a good job finding reinforcements.

I studied the slight Fae man who stood outside. "Who is he?"

"What is the royal historian doing here?" Tarron asked from behind me.

I turned to see his gaze on the man outside, his brow furrowed.

"Ah, he's my partner for recruiting reinforcements," Aeri lied. "He's just waiting for me."

"It's okay, Aeri. I told him." I turned to Tarron. "I told her that I was fated to kill you and asked for her to look for the reason why, considering that we were too busy hunting my mother."

"Well, let's go talk to the man, then." Tarron sounded matter-of-fact about it. He strode toward the door.

Aeri looked at me, brows raised. "He took it rather well."

"I don't know if there is any other way to take it," I whispered. "Hysterics is the only other possible option, and he's not really prone to them, is he?"

"No. Definitely not."

We followed Tarron outside.

The Fae historian's eyes widened when he saw Tarron. He bowed deep, the silver thread on his navy blue coat catching the light. His hair gleamed a similar color. "My lord."

Tarron inclined his head. "What do you have to tell us, Orin?"

I stepped up alongside Tarron, waiting with my breath held.

"Well, ah. You see… There's a royal blade."

"That will be used to kill me?"

"To kill any Fae royal, really." He blinked, his eyes almost owlish despite the fact that he wasn't even wearing glasses. "The woman here"—he gestured to Aeri—"asked me how your death might be able to extinguish the blaze that could devour our kingdom."

"And?" Tarron prodded.

"Well, once she described that you could be stabbed—I knew. There is a special blade. It starts as a normal dagger, but it must be one owned by Fae Royalty."

"Any of my daggers, then," Tarron said.

"Yes. Or any of the Unseelie Queen's. If one were to anoint this dagger in the flames of the Eternal Fire, it would undergo a transformation that would imbue it with the magic to channel a royal's power."

"In what way?" I asked.

"If you were to kill him—or the queen—with a dagger such as this, it would release all of their magic in a blast great enough to blow out the Eternal Fire."

"Just blow it out?" Aeri asked.

"It would be an extremely concussive force. Any person standing in the vicinity would be knocked unconscious, surely."

"But not killed?" Tarron asked.

"No, a normal Fae would not be killed," the historian said. "However, the other Fae royal would also die. The Unseelie and Seelie are two halves of a coin, you see. If the Seelie King is killed with this blade, the true Unseelie ruler will die as well. Two deaths, magically connected."

Oh boy, that was a lot to absorb. But I'd stop all of this before I had to use the dagger on Tarron, so it was a moot point. I just had to believe that.

I met the historian's gaze. "Thank you for the information."

He inclined his head. "I'm off, then." His gaze moved to Tarron. "My lord?"

"You may go. Thank you, Orin."

The Fae disappeared, and I turned to Tarron and Aeri. "We need to get to Mount Chimaera."

Tarron nodded sharply. "I have a transport charm."

"Good." Even with Connor's semi-antidote, I didn't want to risk entering the ether with my own power. I looked at Aeri. "Ready?"

She frowned. "As I'll ever be."

I felt her on that one. What I'd really like was a trip home to shower, nap, and change my clothes. But that wasn't going to happen. It'd only been about six hours since I'd woken in the cavern, but if felt like a lifetime.

Connor stepped outside with a paper bag. He stuck it out toward us. "You have to eat. For strength. And there's a pep-up potion in there for each of you if you haven't been downing them like champs already."

I smiled and took the bag from him. "You're truly the best. Thank you."

He nodded, then ducked back into the shop.

I dug into the bag and handed out the pasties—extra large—and bottles of water. We ate quickly, and I was grateful for the hearty beef and potato. I swigged down the water bottle and followed it up with a small vial of sweet-tasting potion. We'd only had one of these so far, so another would be fine.

Tarron and Aeri took theirs. After the food and magical caffeine, both looked more alert. I certainly felt better.

"Ready?" Tarron dug into his pocket.

"Ready," Aeri and I said.

Tarron threw the transport charm to the ground and

stepped inside. He reached for my hand and gripped it tight. Aeri followed, and the ether sucked the three of us in, spinning us through space.

The ether spit us out a few seconds later, and I stumbled on the dirt. The sun was approaching the horizon here, and a small town sat a couple hundred yards in the distance.

"That has to be it," Tarron said.

"Could you explain exactly what we're doing?" Aeri asked.

I realized that we hadn't updated her on that yet. We'd spent all our time talking about other things. Other justifiably important things.

"The goddesses who guard the location of the Eternal Flame gave us tips on how to reach our goal." We found a road and walked toward it. As we made our way through the brush, I explained everything that had happened with the goddesses in great detail.

"Thank fates you made it to them," Aeri said.

"Not in time, though." The memory still made me angry.

"I'm not so sure about that. Sounds like they'd be dead if it weren't for you."

"Maybe." I wasn't sure that even my mother could kill a goddess, much less four of them. But that damn crystal of hers had really done a number on them.

We reached the road and headed toward the town, which consisted primarily of small, elegant buildings constructed of pale stone. When we reached the village, we stopped at the edge, inspecting it.

Magic sparked on the air, distinct and unavoidable.

"Supernatural town," Tarron said.

"Better for us." I searched for what I thought might be a shepherd's place and spotted a small house at the edge of town that backed up to a big corral full of multi-colored goats. I pointed to it. "That place is as good as any."

"Aye, looks promising." Tarron started toward it.

Aeri and I hung back a few feet, and I watched him walk ahead of us, his stride confident and sure.

Could this really be the man I was fated to?

It sure felt like it.

But had fate really seen fit to give me a noble, powerful, handsome king?

That was a tall order.

He turned to look back at us. "Any particularly reason you are lagging?"

"Not lagging."

"You're the quickest woman I know. You never let anyone get in front of you."

Fair enough. I looped my arm around Aeri's. "Just chatting." I nodded to his legs. "Anyway, you're going really fast and you're six and a half feet tall. Of course you'll cover more ground."

He grunted and turned back. We kept up the pace behind him—which was really swift, actually—and I leaned toward Aeri.

"Do you think the Fae kingdom will have the reinforcements it needs?" I asked.

"I don't know. There were plans to evacuate if you didn't stop the queen, and I'm sure they're enacting them now. But a lot of the Fae can't leave. Some are bound there by magic."

"Against their will?" I was aghast.

"No, not really. Their strength is tied to the place—the young, sick, and elderly, primarily. They rely on the magic of their realm for strength."

"Well, shit." That meant that the Seelie kingdom was full of the most vulnerable. The people we were most required to protect.

If Tarron's death were the only way to stop my mother's fire, he would step right up to the plate.

"Exactly," Aeri said. "As you can imagine, most aren't leaving. Even if they could, they want to stay to protect the others. But how the hell do you protect from a flame that devours everything?"

"You don't." And they had to know it. They'd been familiar with the myth of the Eternal Flame. They knew that staying meant dying, but they wouldn't leave their family behind.

I wouldn't either.

The damned Unseelie Queen.

I wouldn't think of her as my mother anymore. Not if this was what she'd planned—and it so clearly was.

Pain stabbed me through the stomach, and I doubled over, a cold sweat breaking out on my skin. As if in response to my disloyal thoughts, the queen's magic tugged hard at me, compelling me to go to her.

Shit. We'd never gotten a charm to block my transport magic.

Aeri bent and supported me. "Mari! Are you okay?"

"Yeah." I gasped the word.

Out of the corner of my eye, I saw Tarron standing right next to me. He'd clearly seen me double over and had appeared at my side in a second, silent as the grave.

His strong hands gripped my shoulders, supporting me.

I drew in an unsteady breath and straightened. "I'm fine. Just her magic pulling on me."

"It's a doozy, huh?" Aeri asked.

"She doesn't do things in half measures." I felt like it would tear me apart—and that was *with* Connor's potion to lessen the effects.

"Can you walk?" Tarron asked.

The unspoken worry in his tone voiced the second question—are you even capable of this journey?

"I'm fine." I straightened my spine and made sure my voice was sharp. "Let's go. We're nearly there."

We set off again, but this time, Tarron made sure to keep his pace so slow that it was irritating.

"I appreciate your concern," I said. "But don't. We need to do this. I'll be fine. You don't have to worry about me."

His brow furrowed, and he sounded disbelieving. "Not worry about you?"

"He seems to think that's a dumb idea," Aeri translated.

"I get it, Aeri." I shot her a look. "Sisters are just the best."

She grinned.

But his concern warmed me. Despite all the truly horrifying shit that was staring down the barrel at me, that still managed to warm my cold, dead heart.

I sucked in a breath and shoved it aside. There was no time for sentiment. Just action.

We approached a small house, and Tarron knocked on the door. I waited, foot tapping and tension high.

After a few moments, a small man opened the door. His dark hair was curly and his skin a warm brown. Dark eyes sparked with intelligence, and despite his small stature, an aura of danger circled around him.

"I am Tarron. Are you Devrim, the shepherd acquaintance of the four guardians who protect the Flames of Truth."

The man gave us a suspicious look. "Which goddesses would those be?"

"Hestia, Vesta, Brigid, and Arinitti," I said.

"Harrumph. Yes. That is me." His gaze moved to Aeri and me.

"I'm Mordaca." I tried to smile in a friendly way, but I was sure it didn't reach my eyes. Until this was settled, no smile would.

"I am Aerdeca."

He grunted, then gestured us inside. "Come in."

We followed him into a small but impeccably neat

house. He led us to a kitchen, where he began to prepare tea or coffee—I couldn't quite tell which.

"I don't mean to be rude," I said. "But we are in an incredible hurry due to some truly dire circumstances."

"The type of circumstances that could cost the lives of thousands," Tarron said.

The man turned to us. "That is often the case with the Eternal Fire. I presume you would like transportation across the fields?"

"We would, please." I nodded to Tarron.

He reached into his pocket and withdrew the small box, which he presented to the man.

Devrim opened it, his eyes going bright. "The goddesses must truly favor you."

"Or they favor our goal," I said. "Will you help us?"

He nodded. "I will. For this."

"Could we go now?" Tarron asked.

The man looked longingly at the boiling water, then nodded and turned it off. "Yes. If the goddesses gave you this, then I can see that we must leave posthaste."

"Thank you." My shoulders relaxed the smallest amount.

Maybe, with any luck at all, we would stop her.

13

Devrim led us out to the back corral. Dozens of goats shifted in their enclosure, their flaming red eyes turning toward us.

"Those are some interesting goats you have," I said.

"Indeed." He smiled at me. "Rare, Chimaeran goats. Fireproof wool."

One of the goat baahed, and a blast of fire shot from its mouth. The flame flew all the way toward us, and I darted backward, narrowly avoiding the blast.

"Ah, yes. You may want to keep a wary eye out."

I shared a look with Tarron and Aeri. Both eyed the goat speculatively.

"You could probably weaponize them," Aeri murmured.

One of the goats narrowed its beady eyes at her. She raised her hands in a gesture of apology. "Of course not. Sorry, ladies."

The creature baahed and shot its fireball at her. She shifted, then met my gaze. "We need to get the hell out of here. Quickly."

I looked at Devrim, who was leading us toward a dark green open-top jeep parked at the side of the enclosure. "We're going to go through fields of these goats?"

"We are."

"So the only way through, if one doesn't go with you, is by flying?"

He turned and shook his head. "Not really. You'll see."

I raised my brows and nodded, hoping he could tell that I was interested in hearing more. But nope. That was all he had to say, apparently. He turned his attention to readying the jeep.

"He's as enigmatic as the damned goddesses," I muttered.

We climbed into the vehicle, with me and Aeri taking the back. I preferred to be able to stand on the flat bench seat if I needed to do any fighting. Not that the goats would necessarily leap into the jeep, but how was I to know? I'd never seen one that could breathe fire, so they could be capable of anything.

"Seat belts!" Devrim shouted.

I grumbled but put mine on. Aeri did the same.

"Normally I'm all for seat belts," I muttered. "But not when I'm at risk of getting barbecued by a goat."

"How the tables have turned." Devrim chuckled, and I had to assume he was making some kind of mutton cooking joke.

If I hadn't been a complete and total basket case, I might have laughed.

Devrim took off with a hard press of gas. The jeep leapt forward and took off down the street. The crazy shepherd was going a good sixty miles an hour through his little town, and he cranked up the speed when he reached the open road.

Approximately a mile from town, he turned a hard right and headed toward the huge mountain in the distance. The jeep's big tires ate up the ground as he increased the speed, bouncing over lumps in the grass and dipping into potholes. I tightened my grip on the handle above me and peered at the goats who milled around, chomping on grass. Occasionally they'd blast the green stalks with their fire, maybe to give it a little crunch. Every now and again, one would look at us, red eyes flaming.

"Mari, look up." Aeri's voice turned my attention to the sky.

Red clouds swept through the air, which was beginning to turn toward dusk.

"That's not a sunset." Horror formed a pit in my stomach.

"The sky is on fire," Aeri said.

She was right. The red clouds were made of flame.

Devrim turned around, pointing at the clouds as he spoke. "And *that* is why you don't want to fly."

"Then double thanks for the ride." I gripped the handle above my head tighter, hoping this ride ended soon. I'd rather face down a bunch of endangered lions than hang out in the back of this bumpy thing much longer.

We were about halfway toward the mountain when Devrim turned around to meet our eyes. "Get ready."

"For what?" Tarron asked.

"The speed."

"*This* isn't fast?" Shock lanced me. I was familiar with speed. I'd bought my mustang for it. I was no slouch. But… "Aren't we going fast enough?"

"Not for Angry Ahabi." He pointed to a cluster of goats off to our right and a bit forward.

A huge goat in front stared at us, red eyes flaming. She was twice the size of the others, and her posse had to be made up of two hundred other goats.

"Angry Ahabi was once mine. No longer. She has forged off on her own."

Angry Ahabi shrieked, a great baa that sent a shiver down my spine. Then she charged, her head low to the ground and smoke blowing from her nose. The others followed, headed straight for us. The ground trembled with the force of their footfalls, the horde of them moving so fast that they would surely intercept us.

My heart jumped into my throat.

This was not what I had been expecting. Being frightened by goats was so not in my wheelhouse.

But Angry Ahabi was a big bitch, and she plowed ahead with the force of a locomotive. Flames burst from her nostrils, blackening the wool on her chest. She didn't so much as slow. Her minions kept up, so many of them that they could trample us to death.

"Shit, shit, shit." Aeri, who was closest to the goats, unbuckled her seat belt and stood on the seat.

"Hold on!" Devrim yanked on the steering wheel and turned hard left, veering away from the horde.

Tarron stood, his magic rising on the air. The field began to smell of autumn, and he thrust out his hands, throwing a huge blast of water at the goats.

Angry Ahabi's flame doused, and she howled, a baa that it sounded like it came from the depths of hell. She plowed forward, picking up speed.

With her head down and her feet thundering, she was likely planning to ram the front wheels of the car. She moved so fast that she could probably break an axle, then we'd end up crushed under their hooves.

Ah, shit.

Devrim was a great driver, fast and sure. He swerved and accelerated, keeping just out of range of Angry Ahabi, who was slowed by Tarron's jets of water but not enough to stop her. She seemed to be propelled by pure, unadulterated rage. Her minions never slowed up, either, ready to pound us into the ground under their hooves.

I unhooked my seat belt and stood. "Aeri. Let's break open the earth. Tarron, you too."

He nodded, not stopping the flow of water that he was using to slow the goats, who plowed through like freight trains. I cut into my finger, watching Aeri do the same. Pain sliced, then black blood welled. I used my Dragon Blood to imagine breaking the earth apart as a fissure that would separate us from the murderous goats.

Aeri's magic surged, the sound of birdsong cutting through the dusk. Tarron's did as well, and the earth to the right of the jeep began to crack in front of Angry Ahabi.

We created a chasm so wide they couldn't jump it. I held my breath, hoping Angry Ahabi would stop.

I respected that angry goat. She was just protecting her turf. I didn't want her plummeting into a pit.

She skidded to a halt in front of the chasm, her eyes alight with rage. The baa that escaped her made the hair on my arms stand on end. She eyed me with her gleaming gaze, and I waved.

"Maybe next time, Angry Ahabi!" I shouted.

"That goat will come for you," Devrim said.

"I'll need to stay off her turf, then."

He shook his head. "Well done. But you'd best hope she doesn't visit your dreams."

I swallowed hard, giving Angry Ahabi one last look. I liked my beauty sleep—no way I wanted a pissed-off, fire-breathing goat rampaging through my head.

I sat back down, shoving away the concern. Devrim drove the last bit at a fast clip, the jeep bouncing along as we approached the base of the mountain. It was tall and jagged-looking, with scrubby trees and great boulders all along the lower portion.

Devrim pulled the jeep to a halt at the base of the mountain. Fiery red clouds hung low over the slopes. They blew on the wind, traveling faster than normal clouds, sweeping along. Their movements were erratic and impossible to anticipate.

Flying up the side of that mountain would be a *terrible* idea. The clouds would burn my wings to dust in no time. They forced us to take the difficult route overland, making us face off against the protections and predators who prowled the night.

Devrim turned to look at the three of us. "We're here. Follow the path and try not to die."

"Thanks." I hopped out of the car. "We appreciate the ride. Best of luck getting back."

He nodded. "You should be able to transport out of here when you're done, if you have that power. It's not protected against people leaving—only coming. So there's no need to call me."

"We won't," Tarron said, and I got the impression that Devrim really didn't want to do two drives across Angry Ahabi's turf.

"Best of luck." He saluted, then drove off, the jeep's lights glowing red as it disappeared into the night.

The sun had just set, and it was almost fully dark. Not ideal for walking into lion territory, but there was obviously no choice.

"Here's the path." Tarron led the way to the narrow, cleared space through the brush.

I got into step behind him, and we made our way forward, single file. Aeri guarded the back. The fiery clouds from above lit the ground well, providing enough light that we wouldn't need to conjure anything.

Tarron looked at me over his shoulder. "You good?"

"Yeah." I couldn't help but notice how damned handsome he looked in the firelight, while kicking myself at the same time since my mind should *not* be on that. But it would be like not noticing a gorgeous sunset as you rode into battle. You *had* to see it.

We made our way silently up the mountain, moving at a swift jog. We needed to get there as fast as possible, and the only option was to run. Soon, my breath was heaving in my lungs and my thighs ached from the upward slope. The heat from the fiery clouds blasted down at us, making sweat drip down my back and my lips dry.

"I really wish I exercised more," Aeri muttered from behind me.

"Ditto." This was killer.

Eventually, we arrived at a break in the path. What had once been one trail opened up to a clearing and deviated to seven separate trails.

"Shit." I stared at them. Danger radiated from each.

"The goddesses made it clear that there was one safe path." Tarron strode from trailhead to trailhead, inspecting each.

I frowned and looked around. "There has to be a clue of some kind."

The three of us began to search—for what, I had no idea. The moon and fiery clouds were bright enough to provide plenty of light for our search. Trees, rocks, and scrubby brush surrounded the trails, and we stuck primarily to those. I wiped sweat out of my eyes as I hunted, poking through brush that scraped my hands and irritated my skin. It took a good five minutes, but finally, Aeri spoke.

"What about this?" Her voice sounded from several yards behind me.

I turned and joined her at the edge of the clearing. She crouched by a flat square stone that she'd cleared some brush off of. Carefully, she ran her fingertips over the inscriptions.

"Nice find." I crouched and looked at it, frowning at the writing. "Shit. I can't read that. Tarron?"

He approached, brows drawn. He crouched low next to me, moving with the grace of a giant ballet dancer. His frown deepened. "That looks like ancient Greek."

"Can you read it?" Aeri demanded.

"No."

Shit.

It could definitely be directions, but none of us could possibly read ancient Greek. I touched the carvings in the stone, wishing I could understand what they said.

As I ran my hand over the deep incision that marked a word at the edge of the stone, understanding flashed in my mind.

I gasped and jerked my hand away.

"What is it?" Tarron demanded.

"That word said danger."

"You can read it?" Aeri asked. "With your Dragon Blood?"

While it was possible that we could *maybe* magic

ourselves into speaking another language, it wasn't likely that we could do a good enough job to interpret complicated passages. Mind and knowledge magics were harder.

"No. I think Hestia, one of the goddesses who guards this place, gave me the ability to read ancient Greek." I could still remember the warm magic that had filled my mind when she'd touched my arm.

"Well, give it a go," Aeri said impatiently.

I drew in a deep breath of too-warm air and touched the words, starting with the ones at the top. Understanding flowed into my mind, my brain trying to keep up with the surge of information.

It was freaking weird.

"Well?" Aeri prodded.

"Hold your horses." I got to the end of the inscription, then frowned. I looked up at the path. "It says that the one that glows with light is the proper path."

"None of them glow," Tarron said.

"Is there another interpretation for light?" Aeri asked.

"I don't think so." I ran my fingertips over the inscription again, but nothing new came to me.

Damn. That was a bit of a mystery.

I stood and walked toward the paths, inspecting them. Each one looked equivalently dark.

Until I reached the last one.

Glittering gold fireflies flew in the bushes in the distance, about fifty yards up. I hadn't seen them before. Perhaps they'd come out with the sun setting?

I looked back at Tarron and Aeri. "Come check this out."

They walked over.

A smile tugged up at the corner of his lips when he spotted the fireflies. "That must be it."

Aeri ran back to the other trailheads and peered up each one for a few seconds. She returned. "Yep. Only one with fireflies. I say we do it."

I nodded, then started up the path. I took the lead, moving at a swift jog that felt like hell but was the only option. Sweat dripped, sticky and awful, and I winced at the burn in my lungs.

The trees thinned and more boulders took their place the higher we got. The breeze was a bit stronger up there, thank fates, but it was still hot as hell with the flame clouds overhead. I prayed they wouldn't suddenly drop.

When we reached a passage through a section of towering boulders, I slowed. Tension prickled the air, along with the feeling of eyes on me.

"Does it feel like we're being watched?" Aeri asked.

I nodded. "Sure does."

We slowed to a walk, our footsteps silent. More than anything, we needed to be able to sense when danger was coming. Between the lions and snakes, whatever was watching us had to be bad.

"Alert to the right," Tarron murmured. "I don't see it, but I hear it."

Tension crawled along my skin as we walked.

Tumbled boulders towered on either side of us, forcing

us into a path from which there was no escape. We'd have to go forward or back, and lions could definitely come from those directions. Snakes, too. Even worse, the boulders around us formed huge shadowy nooks and crannies for a creature to hide.

My skin tightened as I walked, eerie awareness making every movement huge and every sound as loud as a gun firing.

When I heard the snuffling breath right by my ear, I stiffened, stopping dead in my tracks.

I stood next to a huge boulder, shoulder high and massive.

"Don't move," Tarron murmured.

I didn't need to look to know what was right by my head. I did anyway, carefully turning my eyes toward the snuffling warm breath.

A lion's huge nose was right by my ears, his golden eyes glued to mine. A majestic mane surrounded his big head, and he growled low in his throat.

My heart felt like it shot right out of my chest as I watched him. His huge fangs had to be as long as my hand, and his breath smelled of dead bodies.

Probably because he'd just eaten some and was hungry for more.

Please kill me before you start to eat me.

No. That was a bad attitude.

The enormous claws that curled over the edge of the rock could disembowel me in a second.

I winced.

But he was truly magnificent. So terrifying that my mind buzzed, going blank. The only thought that drifted through was *I'd rather face down Angry Ahabi*.

"I've got you," Tarron said.

I drew in a shallow breath. I could try to blast the lion with some magic, but that would suck. *Endangered Species Killer* was not something I wanted on my resume.

Cold sweat dripped down my back as Tarron rustled behind me. His magic flared slightly on the air. I couldn't see him, but I did catch sight of an enormous steak, bloody and red, as it appeared right in front of my face.

Like a huge kitty treat that he'd conjured.

The lion nipped it right out of Tarron's fingers and chomped it down in just a few bites. Then he stared at me, growling.

"Uh, Tarron?" Aeri said from the very back. "There's another by your head."

The second growl came from behind, to my left. Then a third, a little farther back.

"Now there's one by me." Her voice was no more than a squeak.

Tarron moved carefully but quickly. I could barely hear him, but I saw two more steaks get set on the rock right in front of my lion.

"Aeri's lion," I hissed.

"I'm working on it," he bit out.

The lion gobbled up the steaks then kept staring at me.

Shit. Shit. Shit.

"This isn't working." My skin turned icy with fear as the lion leaned closer. "This is so *not* working."

I stared straight ahead, frozen. He growled so close to my cheek that his whiskers touched me.

Oh, shit.

14

The lion breathed on my face, hot air that reeked of the meat Tarron had fed it.

Yeah, this was so wasn't working.

Cats liked big toys almost as much as they liked food. We could feed it until it was stuffed, and it might still want to bat me around like a giant fuzzy mouse or baby bird.

I didn't want to be either.

I drew in a shuddery breath as my mind raced. Cleverness was the only way out of this, and we needed to hurry the hell up.

"Illusion, Aeri," I murmured. "Antelopes."

I prayed she understood what I meant as I sliced my finger and let my Dragon Blood well. The magic flowed through me, and I called upon it, crafting the illusion of a fat, juicy antelope right in front of me. I had to do it from memory, so even I knew that the creature looked a bit weird. Like an unskilled painter had created it.

I made the antelope run down the path away from us, its hoofs kicking up dust and its butt bouncing. The lion's head swung toward it, and I could see interest glow in its eyes.

The majestic beast leapt off the rock to my right and landed with a graceful thud on the ground in front of me. Hundreds of pounds of muscle rippled under gleaming golden fur. His flowing mane was shot through with red that gleamed under the light of the fiery clouds.

In a heartbeat, he was tearing after the antelope, his strong strides eating up the ground.

A second lion, the one that had been right behind me menacing Tarron, jumped clean over my head. Huge claws glinted in the light as they flew in front of my face, and the giant cat raced after the other one, in pursuit of the wonky antelope.

I staggered backward, a year taken off my life. Tarron caught me, and I turned, spotting Aeri's lion chasing after a third antelope down the back path. It headed down the mountain after a regal-hoofed creature that looked a hell of a lot more like a real antelope than mine had.

"Holy fates, that was close." Tarron gripped me to him with strong hands, pressing the back of my body full length against his front. I could feel the worry in his embrace. Concern for me.

I leaned against him, absorbing a bit of his strength, as trembling overtook me.

"Good idea, Mari," Aeri said. "Though your antelope had a bit of an impressionist feel to it."

I laughed, a shaky sound. "Yeah, he could have gone in a museum."

"Can they catch those creatures?" Tarron asked.

"Not really. Their claws will go straight through."

"That might piss them off."

"I'm hoping they won't care. They just want to play." I looked to my right, spotting the blood stain from the meat. "They've had a full meal anyway, so hopefully they won't be too mad."

Tarron released me, and I stepped forward. "We need to move."

I nodded, dreading the run ahead but determined to get it over with. If those lions came back, pissed off and fangy, we'd be in trouble.

With a resigned groan, I began to run. We plodded endlessly up the mountain. My breath heaved and my pants clung to my sweaty legs.

Ew.

I certainly wasn't used to *that*. But an uphill run under flaming clouds would turn anyone into a swamp monster.

The boulders around us cleared out as we moved higher, all the vegetation beginning to disappear. Finally, I could see the very top of the mountain. It blazed with orange fire, the flames coming right out of the rock. Even more fiery clouds coalesced at the top.

"It's like hell come to earth," Aeri muttered breathlessly.

My worst nightmares, really. If the Christian hell were

real, I had a feeling they might have modeled this place after it. Or vice versa.

We were close to the top—only a few hundred yards—when a dark energy began to fill the air. The earth in front of us moved, shifting and twisting.

I stumbled to a halt, my breath going short. "Holy fates, what's that?"

"Snakes." Tarron's voice carried a dire tone.

I squinted at the writhing mass. It was at least three huge black snakes, uncoiling upon themselves. They were as wide around as I was and at least twenty feet long. Not as big as the huge serpent I'd faced in the Fae trials, but that was probably a bad thing. These guys would be faster as a result. And their fangs were more than big enough to pierce me right through the chest.

Firelight gleamed on their shimmering black skin, which wafted smoke in the same way that Wally's fur did.

"Hell snakes?" Aeri asked. She'd clearly seen the same thing I had.

"It makes sense, I guess." I eyed their three heads, which were turning to look at us.

Fiery red eyes and brilliant white fangs gleamed. Their skin shimmered with magic beneath the smoke that rose up from their bodies.

"What is a hell snake?" Tarron asked.

"Black magic creature." I searched my memory for all that I'd learned of them. "If we kill them, they will return to the underworld. The goddesses must have put them here."

"When Hestia gave you the knowledge of ancient Greek, did she happen to tell you how to defeat these?" Tarron asked.

"No. I don't think they work at the goddesses' command. They were just plopped down here one day, and now they probably strike to kill."

"An effective guard." Tarron drew his long gleaming sword from the ether. "We need to kill quicker."

I nodded, not feeling the least bit guilty. Being figments of dark magic, they wouldn't even feel pain. We just had to injure their corporeal bodies enough to release the black magic and send them back where they'd come from.

Carefully, I drew my bow and arrow from the ether. Aeri drew her mace and began swinging it over her head, working up a rhythm that would allow her to smash in skulls with efficiency and grace.

The snakes hissed and reared up as we approached. I eyed the sky, wondering if I could strike from above.

A fiery cloud wafted with the wind, moving so quickly that I winced.

Yeah, that had to be avoided if at all possible.

I moved right, trying to draw one of the snakes away from the others. We couldn't have two snakes attacking one person—it'd be more than we could manage.

Tarron shot a jet of flame at one snake, who reared up and caught it in his mouth. He seemed to grow bigger as a result, his body thickening and his eyes glowing a brighter red.

Shit.

"Definitely no to flame," Tarron said.

The Thorn Wolf appeared next to me, crouching low and growling up at the snake who loomed over me. I heard Wally hiss from the side, and realized that he'd shown up to watch Aeri's back.

"Wally says they hate water," Aeri said.

Thank fates for the hell cat.

Tarron's magic filled the air, and a jet of water shot from his palm. It nailed the snake closest to me right in the face, making the creature rear back and shoot fire, rage in every quivering muscle.

With my snake distracted, I aimed my bow at the one who loomed over Tarron. Beyond them, Aeri and Wally were leading her snake on a fast chase. They had it under control, so I focused on Tarron's snake. I fired two arrows, one after the other, so fast that my hands were a blur even to my own eyes. Each arrow struck the snake in one of its eyes, blinding it.

It thrashed, giving Tarron time to keep up the assault on my snake. The water hit the snake in the face, and it kept its head up to avoid the spray, dodging and ducking. I stashed my bow and arrow in the ether and called upon my longest sword. Then I lunged, sprinting for the monster.

Burn ran ahead of me, fast and sure. When he reached a spot about ten feet in front of the snake, he spun and crouched low, turning his red gaze to me.

I got the gist immediately.

I reached the Thorn Wolf and leapt onto his back. He

pushed off, hurling me into the air. I directed my blade right at the snake's chest, sending the metal deep into its body. I kept the blade lodged as I fell, allowing the steel to cut the snake open from within.

Black dust burst out of its innards, an explosion of magic that made my eyes water. I slammed them shut, holding my breath. The dark silt rained down on my head, feeling like spiders crawling over my skin.

I landed hard, then rolled, yanking my blade free as I scrambled away. From behind, Burn growled and snapped as he lunged for the snake.

I turned, opening my eyes. The snake was writhing on the ground, black magic seeping from the huge wound in its belly. I sprinted for it, legs aching, and raised my sword high over its neck. I brought it down with a hard strike, severing the head.

A huge poof of dusty dark magic exploded from the snake's neck as it rolled away.

Panting, I caught a scent on the air—putrid night lilies and brimstone.

The queen is here.

Heart thundering, I spun, catching sight of Tarron directing water at his own snake. We needed to take these bastards out fast.

He blasted the blinded creature in the face, making it lunge backward, then turned his assault on Aeri's snake, hitting it with a jet that threw it off track.

She'd managed to hit it several times in the belly, leaving long black wounds that belched dark magic. Wally had somehow managed to jump onto the snake's giant head and was clawing at its eyes. The little black cat managed to take out one of the fiery red orbs before he was thrown to the ground.

Aeri lunged, putting herself between the snake and a shaken Wally. Tarron hit it with water again, driving it back from her.

Burn lunged for the snake that Tarron had blinded, snapping and growling, trying to keep the beast from attacking Tarron while the Fae king protected my sister.

"Aeri!" I shouted, holding my palm up.

She got the signal, raking her thumbnail down her palm with a wince. White blood flared, bright under the moonlight. I cut my own palm, calling upon the lightning within me. It crackled and burned, surging down my arm.

I raised my palm to face hers, and the electric energy shot from my hand, joining the current that she directed at me.

With the electric whip formed between us, I raced toward the snake, darting around Tarron so he wasn't caught on the wrong side of the lightning.

Aeri ran as well, and we sprinted toward the snake, dragging our electric current with it. While the snake was reared up, trying to avoid the water that Tarron shot at it, we sliced it clean through the middle. Both halves of the body flopped hard to the ground, writhing as they shot out blasts of dark magic.

I dodged around them, dropping my hand to kill the

electricity since we were too far from Tarron's snake to use it there.

Tarron had already killed his jets of water and was in the sky, shooting around the snake's blinded head and going for the tail. A fiery cloud shot toward him, as if it were drawn by his presence in the sky.

"Tarron! Behind!" I screamed.

He surged forward faster than I'd ever seen him fly, lunging down with his sword and striking the snake right through the middle. The powerful blow severed the snake's body in two, and the top half dropped to the ground, writhing.

Gone.

They were all gone.

But no time to recover.

"The queen! She's here." A chill raced over my skin.

"I smell her," Tarron growled.

We raced up the last part of the mountain, leaving the bodies behind as they disappeared, heading back to the underworld. Each of us kept our weapons drawn, and Burn and Wally stayed at our sides, galloping along with murder in their eyes.

The top of the mountain was covered in rocks and rubble, crevasses everywhere. Each one burned with flames that shot from within the earth, a sparkling, fiery glow that was both beautiful and terrifying all at once.

With so many huge boulders all around, it was impossible to see the queen. I caught a flash of movement from ahead of me. Pale skin and dark hair.

"There!" I sprinted for the Unseelie.

Closer up, I realized it wasn't her. Not the queen. Another.

Where was she? This one had to be protecting her. I raced closer.

Three Unseelie leapt out from behind a rock, joining the first. All four had eyes glowing with manic light. At least two of them looked to be enchanted, while the others might've been acting of their own accord.

The difficulty of figuring out who was on her side and who wasn't made frustration devour me. I hated that I might hurt one who was unwilling, but so many more would die if I didn't stop her.

I *hated* difficult decisions.

I charged, stashing my sword in the ether and calling on my bow and arrow. It was in my hands when the first pain hit.

I doubled over, feeling like I'd been stabbed in the stomach by the queen's magic. Gasping, I tried to straighten.

"Mari!" Tarron's worried voice penetrated the haze of pain.

"I'm fine!" The words tore from me. "Keep going!"

Finally, I managed to force myself to stand, a nearly overwhelming compulsion to join the queen surging through me.

No.

I straightened and raised my bow, focusing so hard on

the weapon that it became my world. It had to be my world right now.

I aimed at the Unseelie who was farthest away and sent an arrow right through his neck. Tarron was slicing the head off another, and Aeri had crushed a skull with her mace. Wally and Burn tag teamed the fourth one, claws and fangs flying.

Where was she?

Panic raced through me.

This was the final showdown.

It *had* to be. I couldn't let her make it to the Seelie realm—not with the flame.

Screw it.

I called upon my wings and took to the sky. I needed the higher vantage point to find her. Fast. The heat singed my skin.

"From the left, Mari!" Aeri shrieked.

I didn't hesitate or even look—I just darted to the right as fast as I could, skin and wings burning from the proximity to the clouds. I was so close that it felt like I was actually on fire.

I prayed I wasn't.

Tarron would hit me with a jet of water if I was, right? I had to be fine. Though fine was *really* relative in these circumstances.

I darted through the air, avoiding the flaming clouds and trying to spot the queen through the haze of heat.

Finally, I saw her. Regal and elegant in her sleek black dress with an updo that was horribly perfect, she was standing in front of a huge jet of flame that shot from deep within the earth. She held a crystal ball in her hands, directing it toward the flame. The crystal pulsed, absorbing the fire from the mountain.

Shit.

I dived for her, wind tearing at my hair as I pushed myself to the breaking point. The ground rose up to meet me at a horrifying pace. I was an airplane about to crash.

I slammed into the queen, sending her flying backward. The flaming globe flew out of her hands, rolling away. I tumbled with her, the two of us going head over heels as we bounced over the hard ground.

Her black hair flew around her head, and midnight eyes met mine. She shrieked, her claws going for my face. I ducked, calling a dagger from the ether. I gripped it tight and tried to slam it into her ribs.

At the last minute, my hand stilled.

I thrust it forward, but it wouldn't move.

She clawed my face, nails raking. Pain and frustration roared within me. I tried to stab her—tried to thrust the blade forward so it would pierce her stomach.

My arm wouldn't move.

"You can't hurt me," she hissed. "My magic prevents it."

The stupid potion she'd hit me with.

I tried to knee her in the stomach, to see if a weaponless attack would work.

My leg froze.

Shit.

She clawed at my neck. Pain flared. Blood welled. Her strong hand yanked me to her.

"Come with me, daughter." Her words pulled at me, dragging at the magic within my bones. It was so desperate to obey her. Connor's charm suppressed it, but I could still feel it trying to roar to the surface.

A slender dagger slammed into her shoulder, appearing out of nowhere and shocking me out of my trance. She shrieked, her eyes going wide.

Someone had nailed her.

I scrambled back.

Tarron or Aeri hadn't been hit by her damned potion, so their daggers could hit her.

My muscles burned as I fought her grip, trying desperately to get away. I couldn't let her transport out of here with me in her grip, and I definitely didn't want to get in the way of a killing blow.

"You bitch," I hissed, and I did *not* mean it as a compliment this time.

Finally, I managed to break her grasp and crawl away, scrambling over the ground.

In all my life, I'd never hated anything as much as I hated this cowardly retreat. Given the circumstances, it was the only thing I could possibly do, but *I* wanted to be the one fighting.

I lurched to my feet and spun around, catching sight of Tarron shooting an enormous bolt of fire at the queen.

She yanked the dagger out of her shoulder and threw it

aside, then thrust out her hand and diverted the fireball right at Tarron.

He lunged away, taking a hit to his wing but staying on his feet.

Shit.

So *that's* where I'd got that power. My ability to absorb and redirect magic had come directly from her, just like my sense of premonition.

Yet she used it differently.

I needed to learn to do that. My powers were still settling into me. Still morphing. I'd delight in finding a way to use them against her.

Aeri threw another dagger and hit her in the chest. The queen staggered, gasping. Her enraged eyes met Aeri's, and she thrust out her hand.

"No!" I screamed, not knowing what she was going to throw at Aeri.

I lunged in between them, taking the hit straight on. I barely had time to brace myself. The magic crashed into me, a sonic boom that made my insides shake. I directed it back at her. The magic plowed through the air, slamming into her chest and throwing her backward.

She landed right next to the glowing ball of Eternal Flame.

Through bleary eyes, I saw her grab it. She still hadn't removed the dagger from her chest, but her eyes were bright with energy and life.

Aeri's blow had not been a killing one.

I dragged myself to my feet, trying to stagger toward her. To stop her.

But she disappeared, the orange ball of fire clutched in her hand.

No.

I dropped to my knees, pain and horror overtaking me.

15

I knelt on the hard stone, flames blazing around me as I processed what had just happened.

"She got the Eternal Fire." The words whispered were so quiet I could barely hear them.

I looked up, a huge empty space opening inside my chest.

Aeri ran toward me from a distance, but Tarron was closer. Standing right near me. He strode toward me, his brow set.

Terror like I'd never known gripped me. It felt like I was on trial with the punishment to be immediately served after—and I'd just been sentenced to death.

But it wasn't my death.

It was Tarron's.

I staggered upright. "I'm sorry."

"It's not done yet." His firm tone—so confident and

sure—buoyed me slightly in the horror of what could come to pass.

I sucked in a deep breath.

Freaking out wasn't my style.

Being crippled by fear wasn't my style.

Extenuating circumstances or not, I just wasn't here for this. That wasn't me.

Another steady breath returned half of my brain. Or at least, that's what it felt like. I stared at Tarron, thoughts racing through my mind. Plans.

We had to kill her with the blade. It was the only way. Her death would serve just as well.

No. It wouldn't. When the blade released its massive burst of energy, it would kill the nearest Fae royal.

Him.

No matter what, if this blade were used, he and the Unseelie queen would die. They were two halves of a whole—Seelie and Unseelie. The royals from both sides.

Not an option.

"We have to get to your realm. Kill her before she releases the fire," I said.

He nodded sharply. "I'll alert the Court Guard."

I turned and ran toward the blade that the queen had thrown to the side. When I bent to pick it up, I spotted the telltale sign of black Unseelie blood.

"Got you, you bitch." A dark smile crept across my face as I grabbed it.

"Her blood?" Aeri asked.

"Yeah. I'll get the antidote, then I'll be able to attack her." *I* wanted to be the one who took her out.

"What is Tarron doing?" Aeri frowned at him behind me.

I turned, spotting him leaning over one of the blasts of Eternal Flame, holding his dagger into the fire.

I stalked toward him. "What are you doing?"

"Preparing."

"For your death?" Fear and rage collided within me. Both feelings so frantic, so amorphous, that I couldn't control them.

"Or hers."

My heart tore in two. "It's *both* of yours. If one Fae royal is killed with this, the other one dies. Two halves of the coin—Seelie and Unseelie."

"I know." His voice was calm. Not afraid. Not stressed. Not angry.

My lips thinned as I growled at him. I didn't even want to think that it was a possibility.

And yet he was preparing for it.

"Let's go." He shook the dagger a bit to try to cool it. "We need to get to P & P."

I nodded, hoping that Connor would have the potion ready to go. We had almost no time to spare, but with the queen injured, there would hopefully be just enough to get me the antidote so I could actually be part of the fight instead of a bystander.

Not only did I want to be the one to take her out…I had

a feeling that I would have to be. There was something about our magic, about our bond. It would have to be me.

Aeri joined Tarron and me.

He pulled a transport charm from his pocket and looked at us. "Ready?"

I nodded, resolute.

He tossed the charm to the ground, and a silver cloud exploded upward. He gripped my hand, and we stepped in. The ether sucked me in, spinning in a whirlwind.

A moment later, we stepped out on the sidewalk in front of P & P. It was midday now, and finally, it hit me exactly how tired I was. The pep-up potion was starting to wear off, and I was almost woozy from exhaustion. The temperature change had to have something to do with it. It'd been hot as blazes at Mount Chimaera, and it was far cooler here.

I stepped toward the door, entering a scene of chaos inside P & P. Paper bags sat on every surface, and the air was thick with the savory scent of pasties. Connor bustled around, filling bags with pasties fresh from a tray, while Claire piled the bags into big boxes. She was dressed in her all-black fight wear with her hair pulled back, and she was moving as fast as a sprite.

"What's going on?" I asked.

Connor looked up. "Packing for the fighters."

"The ones in my realm?" Tarron asked.

"The same. With a battle about to start, there isn't exactly a ton of time for food prep in the Seelie Court."

"True enough, but how did you know the battle would happen?"

Connor shrugged, his black shirt covered in flour. "Didn't. But it can't help to be prepared."

"Not to mention that prep work for the battle has exhausted everyone," Claire said. "They'll need to eat whether we're fighting or not." Her brows dropped. "Hang on a second... Is the battle going to happen? Do you have confirmation?"

"I'm afraid so," Tarron said. "I've already alerted the Court Guard. They're moving the infirm, young, and elderly to the sky platform."

I turned to him. "Sky platform?"

"It's a huge platform high in the sky, enchanted with fairy lights to float over the town. It was the best way to get the non-fighters away from anything that could burn."

"You've been busy." Respect swelled within me. He'd only been out of my sight for a few minutes here and there, yet he had somehow managed to get that done? He'd delegated it, but still... I was impressed.

"It won't work forever. The fire will devour the whole realm—the platform, too, if we let it burn long enough. But it will buy us time."

Aeri looked up from where she'd started filling boxes. "Better to lose buildings than people."

"Hopefully we won't lose either," Tarron said.

I could tell from his tone that he didn't really believe that. We'd tried repeatedly to stop the queen, and she'd been faster and stronger than us each time.

Shaking away the negative thoughts, I turned to Connor and held out the bloody sword. "I have her blood. Is there any chance that potion is ready? I can't hurt her as long as I'm under its influences."

Connor's eyes brightened. "Yes. I just have to mix it in with the one you already took."

I handed over the blade, and he disappeared into the back of the shop. Tension tightened my muscles as I helped Claire pack up the rest of the boxes. Tarron pitched in, too, and it was done in no time.

Connor joined us a few moments later, a small vial in his hand. My eyes went immediately to it, and I reached out. He handed it over.

"Thank you so much." I swigged it back as he nodded, shuddering at the disgusting taste of sour rot.

Drinking the queen's blood—even a little bit—made me want to gag.

No choice though.

I finished it and looked up. "Well, that was disgusting."

"Do you feel any better?" Tarron asked.

I tilted my head, trying to decide. Then I doubled over in pain, the potion finally getting to me. Gasping, I went to my knees. Tarron knelt beside me, concern creasing his face as he helped support me, his strong arms around my shoulders and waist.

"What's wrong?" he demanded of Connor, concern thick in his voice.

"The poison is leaving her body."

"Will it be over soon?" Tarron asked.

Through the buzzing in my head, I heard Connor answer, "It should be."

The pain faded a moment later. My skin felt clammy, and I looked down at my hand. It was covered in tiny pinpricks of black that had seeped out of my pores.

"Ew."

"You can get cleaned up in the bathroom," Connor said. "There are some towels under the sink."

Shakily, I rose with Tarron's help. I did feel better, despite the weakness. It was as if an extra weight had been removed from my shoulders. Her influence was gone.

"I'll be quick."

Tarron followed me to the bathroom, conjuring clothes along the way. He handed them to me.

"Thank you." I took the bundle of clothes, then disappeared inside the bathroom. "It's like having a walking closet with you."

"Any time."

Quick as I could, I stripped out of my dirty clothes and shoved them in the waste bin, then retrieved a towel from under the sink and dampened it. I wiped myself off as best I could, removing the poison from my skin. I'd kill for a shower, but there was definitely no time.

Finished, I tossed the towel in the bin, then pulled out the trash bag and tied it up so no one would come in contact with the poison that had leached out of me. It was probably inert by now, but still... I wouldn't wish the queen's influence on my worst enemy.

I dressed in the clothes and boots Tarron had conjured

—identical to all my other ones, thank fates—and returned to the people waiting in the bar.

"Ready to go?" Tarron asked.

"Ready."

"First, another pep-up potion." Connor held up three little vials. "How many have you had recently?"

"Two."

He nodded. "Three should be fine. But no more."

"Thank you." I took the magical equivalent of an energy drink from him and swigged it back.

Strength surged through my muscles and alertness through my mind. Tarron and Aeri looked healthier as well.

Two Seelie Fae walked into the shop, their skin luminous and their pale hair pulled back into braids that would be perfect for fighting. Each wore leather armor and slinky chain mail that gleamed in the light.

"That's our ride," Claire said.

Connor hurried behind the counter and grabbed his potions sack.

"You're coming, too?" I asked.

"Wouldn't dream of missing the fight."

"You could burn to death in a fiery blaze of Eternal Fire, you know."

He just shrugged. "If it's my time, it's my time. Wouldn't miss a fight when a friend needs me."

My eyes prickled hotly, and I turned, managing to croak out a quick, "Thanks."

If I survived this, I owed all my friends. Big time.

Though I had a feeling they wouldn't accept it. It wasn't really a payback situation. They did it because they wanted to, and no other reason.

The Fae picked up the boxes of food, and Connor and Claire followed them from the house.

"Let's go." Tarron reached for my hand, then for Aeri's.

We each gripped his hand, and he transported us to the Seelie realm using his specific brand of transportation magic. The three of us spun through space, and the ether spit us out at the edge of town, right underneath an enormous floating platform.

I looked up, craning my neck. "Whoa."

Millions of fairy lights glittered beneath the platform, gleaming bright and golden. Somehow they managed to support it a hundred feet above the ground.

"Mordaca! You're here!" Cass's voice sounded from the right.

I turned to see her loping toward me, Del and Nix at her side. A few yards behind them, Aiden, Roarke, and Ares stood. They were the Origin, the Warden of the Underworld, and Vampire royalty, in that order. Each was hooked up with one of the FireSouls, and even they had come to fight.

"So this thing is going down, huh?" Cass said as she stopped in front of me.

"Yep."

She squeezed my shoulder. "Good luck. We'll be on the east entrance if you need us."

"Thank you."

Everyone would be stationed at the various closed entry points to the realm. They were the most likely places for the queen to try to break through. When she did, reinforcements would flow toward her and the other Unseelie.

"I'm going to go with them," Aeri said.

I gave her a hard hug. "Be careful. If it gets too dicey, leave." I looked at the FireSouls. "Same goes for you."

"Sure." Aeri said, and I didn't believe a word of it.

The FireSouls nodded their heads yes, but their eyes said no.

They'd stay, no matter how iffy it got.

The group all turned and retreated, heading toward their post. A monster truck drove up alongside them, three women leaning out. Two brunettes and a blonde—the DragonGods from the Undercover Protectorate in Scotland. More friends, who I hadn't seen in ages. Here to help. They waved at us as they picked up the FireSouls and my sister, then zoomed off toward the east, the big truck eating up the ground.

I turned to look at Tarron.

"You have a lot of friends," he said.

I nodded, my throat a bit tight. Was that what you called people who risked their lives for you?

It seemed like there should be a better word, though I couldn't think of it.

"Let's get going." I looked up. "Will we wait up there?"

He nodded. "It's equidistant from all the entrances, so when she arrives, we're most likely to get to her quickly."

I drew in a deep breath and called upon my wings,

eying the dagger sheathed at Tarron's thigh as I rose high into the air. He flew alongside, graceful and powerful on the air.

We landed on the edge of the platform, and guilt swelled inside of me at the sight of all the scared faces. The Fae—old, young, and sick—all sat on mats and cushions, waiting.

This had to be what the Tube tunnels had looked like in London during the Blitz.

Barbaric.

I made my life out of violence—chasing demon hunters and pretty much bathing in their blood daily.

But that was small scale, and it was my choice.

This garbage...

War.

"It's bullshit," I muttered.

Tarron squeezed my hand, and I had a feeling he knew what I meant by it.

I turned from the faces, needing to center myself. I couldn't be freaking out when the queen showed up—that was a recipe for losing. And this was one fight—*the* one fight—I couldn't afford to lose.

The entire perimeter of the platform was populated by warrior Fae, wings at the ready. Armor gleamed in the sun, and weapons glinted menacingly. The land-bound enforcements were situated on the ground, whereas those who could fly would attack from the air, launching off of this platform.

Tarron made the rounds, speaking to the soldiers.

Bolstering them. Their shoulders straightened after a few words from him, and it was clear what kind of king he was.

The best.

The kind who would die for his people, all while letting them believe he'd usurped the throne from his brother so he could protect the legacy of his loved one.

Finally, he joined me, and we stood, staring out at his kingdom.

Wind blew my hair back from my face, and I shivered.

It truly was beautiful. The entire place looked like a fairy tale—but then, that's where the term probably came from.

Tension tightened my skin as we waited. I had no idea how long it could be.

"In all honesty, she could wait days," I said.

"She could."

"I don't think she will. I don't think she *can* wait."

"Agreed." Tarron squeezed my hand, and I wondered if this would be the last time we'd touch each other.

Was our fated mate bond meant to end like this? Short, volatile, passionate—and then one meant to kill the other?

It was too horrible to even contemplate.

I shook my head, driving away the fear.

There was no way I'd let fear take me now.

"She just has to heal, then she'll be here." If I went to her, would she stop this?

No.

And she'd cause far more damage than this. With me as her weapon, the whole world was at risk.

I'd no sooner thought it than it felt like the world itself exploded. From the east, a massive blast thundered through the air, knocking back our fighters.

"It is time," Tarron bellowed.

Instinct overrode my terror of what was to come, and I was grateful. I'd spent very little of my adult life being afraid—I was entirely unused to it.

Tarron turned to me and gave me one last kiss on the lips. Hard, fast, full of feeling.

Then over.

He pulled away and launched himself into the sky. I took to the air, my wings flaring wide and carrying me swiftly over the ground below. Tarron stuck close to my side, and hundreds of Seelie flew all around.

The queen and her Unseelie forces were pouring out of a portal in the middle of a field. They were a good hundred yards from the nearest building. They'd need to reach it to allow their flame to alight. Tarron had mentioned that they'd left this entrance—the one farthest from the city—just a tiny bit weaker than the rest. They'd shored up everything to the best of their ability, but when magic ran short, this was the one chosen to be faulty.

And it had worked. The weakness in the protections had drawn the queen, and she'd chosen to break through here.

It gave us more time to take her out before she could light the city on fire.

I swooped toward the Unseelie, who were launching themselves into the sky. Black hair and pale skin was stark against the blue, cloudless backdrop. Many of them stayed on the ground, surrounding the queen. She would stay there, I was sure—more protection when you were standing. No one could attack you from below.

Our side collided with theirs in a clash of magic and metal.

I spotted an enormous crow soaring through the air, grabbing an Unseelie in its talons. It had to be Ana, the Morrigan, a Dragon God who represented the Celtic pantheon. Nearby, Cass flew in her griffon form. Huge and majestic, she had golden feathers that transitioned to fur, huge claws and a beak that could crush horses. She went for the Unseelie, snapping at the wings with her jaws. Behind her, I spotted the Origin. The first original shifter also preferred the griffon form. He was even bigger than Cass, able to grab two Unseelie at a time with his front claws.

Tarron shot into the battle, flying ahead of me and colliding with an enemy, sword to sword. Their blades clashed and blood flew. Tarron fought with a force and speed that was difficult to comprehend.

I looked to the ground, trying to find an open space around the queen. I didn't need a lot of room—just enough to attack from. I gave my transportation power one go, trying to reach the spot right next to her, but it didn't work.

Damn it.

There had to be some kind of magical barrier, and I

wasn't surprised. She wouldn't come here and leave herself open like that.

I eyed the area around the queen, looking for my in. Dozens of Unseelie pointed arrows at the sky, ready to fire should we approach.

Del, on the ground below, danced through the crowd of Unseelie in her phantom form. Transparent blue and incorporeal, she passed right through them, turning solid only briefly so she could stab one in the shoulder. Nix stood on the outskirts farther away, firing arrows at a record pace, taking out Unseelie after Unseelie.

I couldn't help feeling guilt at the deaths of those who weren't willingly serving the queen, and I hoped that Nix wasn't shooting to kill. I'd asked Aeri to explain to everyone what the deal was. Fortunately, it looked like Nix was aiming for legs and shoulders—debilitating but not killing.

I looked closely. Everyone was doing that, in fact. In a battle like this, it was impossibly difficult to pull your punches and only wound when your enemy was determined to kill, but the magical might of those assembled here was phenomenal. If anyone was up to the task, it was my friends.

The Seelie warriors were more vicious, however, and I couldn't blame them. They had no reason to believe me when I said that some of these fighters were unwilling. And behind them was a platform full of their weakest loved ones waiting to be burned to death.

If I were in their shoes, I'd probably kill first and ask questions later as well.

Aeri fought on the ground below, swinging her mace with terrifying accuracy and nailing the Unseelie in the arms. She was chopping them away from the herd, getting closer and closer to the queen.

Even as our forces broke down the queen's guard, the evil one moved ever forward toward the town. Her horde was like a steam engine, rolling ever onward. They lost dozens of their number, falling to my friends' magic and metal, but they kept going. Tarron fought bravely from the other side, cutting down Unseelie after Unseelie. But there were so many.

Finally, I spotted my chance.

And she was nearly within throwing distance of the closest building. There was no time left. I called a small shield from the ether and charged, headed straight for the queen.

Straight for death.

16

I HURTLED THROUGH THE SKY TOWARD THE QUEEN, MY HAIR whipping back in the wind. The short dagger in my hand felt like a lifeline. It wasn't the enchanted dagger—no way in hell was I using that one.

The queen's eyes caught on me and she shrieked. She launched herself into the air, headed right toward me. I hurled my blade, aiming right for her stomach.

She jerked out of the way at the last minute, and the dagger went sailing by. I called upon another and sent it flying harder toward her.

In the distance, I caught sight of Tarron trying to fight his way to me, but I turned my attention toward the queen.

She hurled a blast of magic at me, and I deflected it with my sword. More Seelie were flying to her, trying to reach her from all angles.

It has to be me.

I threw my second dagger with such force and precision that it had to land.

It has to.

The blade flipped through the air as it flew. She darted right, swift and graceful. All the same, it nailed her in the side. She shrieked, clutching her ribs with her free hand. Black blood poured through her fingers.

I raced for her, drawing a sword from the ether. In seconds, I was on her, my eyes glued to the glass ball of fire in her hand. I slashed my blade toward her shoulder, not daring to hit the arm that held the ball. I would have to grab it before it fell. It probably wouldn't alight on the damp grass below, but I couldn't take the risk.

At the last second, she drew a blade from the ether and parried. Our swords clashed in the air, and I kicked at her stomach, trying to force her to lose her balance.

She darted, narrowly avoiding my blow, and I drew my sword back. I struck out for her again and kicked the dagger that was still lodged in her side.

She howled, pain and rage in the sound, then flew for me, impossibly fast. Her foot plowed into my stomach, sending me tumbling back through the air. I went head over heels from the force of her blow, narrowly managing to stop myself before I slammed into the ground.

Even with my newfound ability to actually land a hit on her without being stopped by magic, she was still more powerful than me.

As I flew toward her, wings weak and muscles aching, I knew I needed to be cleverer to beat her.

What about the reflecting magic? She used it differently than I did. I just needed to find a new way to use it to strike back at her.

She was nearly to the buildings now, though. I threw another dagger. I didn't dare try for the bow. It required me to pause and aim, and I didn't have that kind of time. My blade managed to hit her in the arm when she wasn't looking. She hissed and turned to me, rage shining in her dark eyes.

I was nearly to her. So close.

She threw the fireball.

Horror swallowed me whole as I watched it sail toward the nearest building and explode against the roof. Flames burst to life, licking over the surface.

No.

No!

Anger and terror exploded within me, giving me a powerful burst of energy that shot me forward.

I will kill her.

Rage drove my actions. Not thought. Not rationality. Pure, unadulterated rage and fear like nothing I'd ever felt before.

The Unseelie held off any other attackers who might come at her, and it was almost like they were letting me through. In the distance, Tarron fought viciously to reach her. His blade flew, and blood sprayed as he cut down Unseelie after Unseelie.

But my path was clear.

My mother—the queen—wanted a showdown with me.

She hurled a bolt of magic, and I dodged, going right and then forward, using every inch of Dragon Blood speed I had.

We collided in midair once again, our swords clashing. I slashed for her, determined to take her head off.

She dodged, slicing my arm with her blade. The steel cut deep, and I nearly dropped my own sword. Blood poured down my arm.

I struck again, nailing her in the leg. The cut was long and deep, and she hissed. She kicked out with her other leg, hitting me so hard that I tumbled backward in the air. She had a strength unlike any I'd ever experienced. I slammed to the ground, agony everywhere.

Dazed, I stared up at the sky. Pain nearly blinded me, but it was the heat of the nearby fire that made terror drive me to my knees. Red, blue, and green—it flickered across the rooftops, devouring and rising high.

Tarron landed next to me, his face white and his lips tight. In the distance, the queen turned on the air and began to retreat.

My heart thundered so loud and so fast that it felt like it would explode. My head roared. Fear chilled me.

My gaze moved to Tarron. "No!"

Jaw set, he removed the blade from the holster at his side.

"No!" Grief tore at my chest.

"You have to."

"No! There's another way." My gaze moved to the queen. This couldn't be happening. It couldn't be time. "I can kill her."

"It will still kill me."

He was right. He was rational. Both Fae royalty would die when this blade was used. Two halves of the same coin, taken out by the magic that was destroying this place.

Panicked, my gaze flashed to him. "This can't be happening."

Somehow, he found the time—the strength—for a tender smile. "It's over, Mari." His gaze flicked up toward the platform in the sky. "Look—the flame is nearly to the platform. They will all die. *All* of them."

My gaze flicked upward, but it was nearly impossible to see through the tears that filled my eyes and the smoke that clouded the air.

The inferno had grown impossibly high, reaching for the sky platform as if it knew the living ones were there. It wanted to burn flesh, not just wood and stone.

I failed.

All I'd wanted was to save Tarron.

My fated one.

I failed.

"But I tried to *stop* this!" I cried.

"I know." He kissed me gently on the lips, and I clung to him, unwilling to let him go. To let time pass.

But it would pass—no matter what we did. Delaying would only cause grief.

I didn't need to be rational though. Tarron did it for me. He pressed the blade into my hand.

My skin grew cold and my stomach lurched. I wanted to hurl the blade away from me, break it in half.

He twisted it so the tip pressed to his chest. Right where his heart was. He did all the work. I could barely see through the tears.

This was what I had seen in my vision.

So perfectly.

Except I hadn't seen him basically killing himself.

Anything for his people.

"Don't leave me." My voice broke.

"I have to." His gaze flicked to the sky platform. "It's nearly there. Only a few feet to go. Most of them can't fly."

I sobbed, the memory of their faces flashing in my mind. Terror like I'd never known opened a hole in my chest.

The queen was nearly to the exit. The Seelie were near death.

And then Tarron did it for me. Though my hands touched the hilt of the dagger, it was he who actually drove it into his chest.

It was the most terrible moment of my life. I could break every bone in my body and nothing would feel as bad as that blade in my hand as I shoved it into the heart of my fated mate.

He stiffened, not even gasping.

For me.

He wouldn't show pain for me.

Somehow, I knew it.

Because of my visions, we assumed I'd been the one to do it. But I hadn't seen our hands clearly. Hadn't realized this would be what happened.

But Tarron had realized. He'd done it.

As he sagged, I screamed, so enraged and grief-stricken that I couldn't hold it in anymore. As the life faded from him, magic exploded out from his body. So much power that it slammed me off my feet.

Barely conscious, I sprawled on the ground, staring up at the flame that began to die down.

I gasped hard, raggedly, refusing to pass out. I crawled to him. Through bleary vision, I spotted the other Fae falling. The blast knocked them unconscious. I fought it with all I had, using every bit of my Dragon Blood strength. I wouldn't be unconscious for Tarron's last seconds on earth.

All around, the flames died. His magic extinguished them in a heartbeat. They faded a few feet before they reached the sky platform. The town turned black instead of orange with flame.

I could no longer see the queen, but I didn't care what happened to her.

I had to get to Tarron.

Impossibly weak, I clawed my way across the ground. His magic still blasted out of him, a golden glow that made my very bones shake.

No.

This couldn't be.

I grew weaker and weaker as I crawled toward him.

Somehow, my life was seeping from me. I could feel it as I grew colder.

I'm dying.

I didn't understand how—the blast of his magic wasn't supposed to kill those it hit, and I could feel the life all around us. The others were unconscious, but not dead.

I didn't care.

I didn't care about anything except getting back to Tarron.

Finally, I reached him, grabbing his limp hand. Not dead. Not yet.

So close though.

Instinct drove me.

I used my new reflective magic, having no idea what I was doing but not caring. I tried to absorb as much of his power as I could—tried to suck it out of the air itself.

The flames were out, and his magic still hovered in the air. He needed that magic—needed it to survive.

He lay limp on the ground as I draped myself over him, sobbing and trying to shove his magic back into him.

The cold crept over me even more as I tried to absorb the power like I had back at the goddesses' temple. I'd stepped into the crystal's electric current and absorbed it, then sent it at the queen.

I could do this.

I sliced my finger with my thumbnail, letting the blood well as I called on my Dragon Blood power. I used it to enhance my Unseelie magic, to help me absorb all the magic in the air so I could force it back into Tarron.

But the cold…

It seeped through me, icing in my veins and turning my movements slow and groggy.

Tarron's eyes were closed, his breathing so shallow that he had to be nearly dead.

I used every magic I had, working on instinct alone, but it wasn't enough. The cold crept ever closer, wrapping me in its terrible embrace.

∽

There was no pain as I opened my eyes. Blinking, I stared up at the cloudy sky.

No, not a cloudy sky.

The entire place was full of clouds.

Was I having a premonition again?

Now?

Wait, when was now?

Confusion tore through me, memories blasting into my mind.

Fire. The queen. *Tarron.*

Gasping, I sat upright. My body felt weightless. There was no pain, no tiredness. Tarron lay next to me.

I fell on him, trying to shake his shoulders to wake him up.

My hands passed right through.

Oh shit.

Tarron opened his eyes, confusion in the depths. Only then did I realize that he was slightly transparent.

I blinked, shocked. "Holy fates. We're *both* dead."

"What did you do?" He sat upright, fast and sure, his tone demanding. He gripped my arms, but was unable to make contact. His hands disappeared right through. "Mari. What did you do? You shouldn't have died! My magic should have only knocked you unconscious."

"I don't know!" Panic flared in my chest. "I did a lot of things. New magic, old magic. Whatever I could to keep you from dying."

Despair flashed across his face. "And it killed you, too."

I reached for him, though my hands couldn't make contact. I was confused and shocked and terrified and almost a bit happy. Every emotion in the universe flashed through me, and I'd never been so baffled in my life.

I didn't want to be dead, but apparently I didn't want to be separated from him either.

I was just grateful to be looking at him. Talking to him. "I don't know what's going on."

He stood and I rose to join him. We looked around, silent.

White clouds. White trees, white grass. It was all ephemeral and pale.

"I'm not really religious, so I have no idea what the afterlife looks like," I said.

"Not this," Tarron said. "This is something else…"

"Are we not dead?"

"I don't—"

"You are not dead." A voice sounded from the right. "Not quite, at least."

I spun, spotting the red-haired Celtic goddess. "Brigid."

She approached, a serene smile on her face. "This is very strange indeed."

"What's going on?" Tarron demanded. "Are my people safe? Is the Unseelie Queen dead?"

Brigid looked at me. "Do you feel dead?"

"What?" Confusion flickered.

"The Unseelie Queen," Tarron said. "Not Mari."

"Mari is the true ruler of the Unseelie."

Holy shit. That was the same language the historian had used. *The true ruler.*

"What do you mean?" I asked, chills racing over me.

"Your mother does not rightfully hold the throne that should be yours."

Horror threatened to devour me. "She's still alive, isn't she?"

Tarron's magic hadn't killed her, because it had killed *me*.

I was the other Fae royalty. Therefore, *I* had bitten the dust when he had.

Brigid nodded. "That Fae is still alive, yes. Injured, but she will survive."

Oh fates. This was so bad. "But the Seelie realm isn't on fire, right?" I asked. "I *saw* the blaze go out."

I wouldn't have tried to shove Tarron's magic back into him if it hadn't done its most important work. He never would have forgiven me.

"It is out, yes. And we Guardians will find a way to extinguish it at Mount Chimaera once and for all, so that this cannot happen again." Her eyes turned dark. "Our hubris got the better of us, thinking that we could protect it. We cannot. Not from one such as she."

My mother. Not the queen at all, in fact.

"What are we?" I asked. "If we're not quite dead."

And how do we get Undead?

"I'm not really sure," Brigid said. "You did something with your magic that has never been seen before. In trying to save Tarron's life, you somehow saved your own as well. Almost."

Tarron gripped my hand.

"Is it because we're fated mates?" I asked.

"That could have something to do with it."

"How can we come back to life?" I demanded. "We have to go back and stop her."

Brigid nodded. "I suppose it is possible, since you aren't really dead. Just a *little* bit dead—your souls trapped at this halfway point."

"What should we do?" Tarron asked.

She shrugged. "You will have to figure that out for yourselves." She gestured around at the white mist. "Find your way through this half realm. Use your wits to reach the other side. Only then can you stop the false queen and save your people."

And with that, she disappeared.

Tarron and I turned to look at each other. Dead. But not quite.

I reached for him. Our hands drifted right through each other, but I felt a surge of comfort.

We'd get out of this.

We had to.

~~~

Thank you for reading *Queen of the Fae!* The next book will be here in early October 2019. Click here to keep the adventure going with Aeri's story!

THANK YOU FOR READING!

I hope you enjoyed reading this book as much as I enjoyed writing it. Reviews are *so* helpful to authors. I really appreciate all reviews, both positive and negative. If you want to leave one, you can do so on Amazon or GoodReads.

AUTHOR'S NOTE

Thank you for reading *Queen of the Fae!* If you've read any of my other books, you might know that I like to include historical places and mythological elements. I always discuss them in the author's note.

I drew quite a lot of inspiration from myth in *Queen of the Fae*. One of the main elements is Eternal Flame. There are many places in the world where eternal flames have burned for hundreds or thousands of years. Some of these are natural phenomena and others are tended by humans, usually as part of a culturally significant ritual. I had quite a few options to choose from for the book and decided to go with the eternal flame at Mount Chimera in Turkey. It has been burning for over 2,500 years and is the largest known venting of methane gas on earth. The fires burn along the mountaintop and were once used as a navigation beacons.

Mount Chimera was often written about by ancient

philosophers and scholars. The Chimera monster is indeed related to the mountain. Most ancient sources, including Homer, record the monster as being the one that we are most familiar with in modern day—the odd creature with a lion's head, a snake's tail, and a goat head protruding from the back. However, other historians described Mount Chimera as being populated by goats, lions, and snakes in different areas. It was his interpretation that I used for the story.

The four goddesses who guard the flame are all ancient goddesses of fire in some sense. The Vestal Virgins once tended the sacred flame of the goddess Vesta, but I thought they were due for a little liberation.

The cave hideout where Tarron and Mari spent the night to avoid the storm is based upon the Lycian rock cut tombs of the Dalyan that were built in the 14th-15th century BC in Turkey. They are an incredible archaeological site that I had no idea existed until I found it on Google, and it just impressed upon me how many amazing sites there are that most of us don't know about. Even though I studied archaeology for years, there are so many amazing wonders that I stumble upon.

The Asiatic lions that almost attack Tarron, Mari, and Aeri while they are approaching Mount Chimera are based upon the real Asiatic lions that went extinct in the 19th century due to human hunting and interference.

Finally, the dagger that Tarron anoints in the Eternal Flame was inspired by a sacred kris dagger from the 15th century Denmark Sultanate in Indonesia. The dagger was said to have been forged in the Mrapen flame, another ever-burning fire that is sacred in Javanese culture.

I think that's it for the history and mythology in *Queen of the Fae*. I hope you enjoyed it and will come back for more Mordaca and Aerdeca.

ACKNOWLEDGMENTS

Thank you, Ben, for everything. There would be no books without you.

Thank you to Jena O'Connor and Lindsey Loucks for your excellent editing. The book is immensely better because of you! Thank you to Aisha Panjwaneey for your helpful comments about typos.

Thank you to Orina Kafe for the beautiful cover art.

ABOUT LINSEY

Before becoming a writer, Linsey Hall was a nautical archaeologist who studied shipwrecks from Hawaii and the Yukon to the UK and the Mediterranean. She credits fantasy and historical romances with her love of history and her career as an archaeologist. After a decade of tromping around the globe in search of old bits of stuff that people left lying about, she settled down and started penning her own romance novels. Her Dragon's Gift series draws upon her love of history and the paranormal elements that she can't help but include.

COPYRIGHT

This is a work of fiction. All reference to events, persons, and locale are used fictitiously, except where documented in historical record. Names, characters, and places are products of the author's imagination, and any resemblance to actual events, locales, or persons, living or dead, is coincidental.

Copyright 2019 by Linsey Hall
Published by Bonnie Doon Press LLC
All rights reserved, including the right of reproduction in whole or in part in any form, except in instances of quotation used in critical articles or book review. Where such permission is sufficient, the author grants the right to strip any DRM which may be applied to this work.

Linsey@LinseyHall.com
www.LinseyHall.com
https://www.facebook.com/LinseyHallAuthor

Printed in Poland
by Amazon Fulfillment
Poland Sp. z o.o., Wrocław